The TRUTHER ROOSTER

A FICTIONALIZED STORY ABOUT HOW TO INCREASE HUMAN OKNESS IN I'M OK—YOU'RE OK ADULT-ADULT GAME-FREE DIALECTICAL DEMOCRATIC DISCUSSIONS

RICHARD JOHN STAPLETON

Inks and Bindings
888-290-5218
www.inksandbindings.com
orders@inksandbindings.com

CONTENTS

OVERVIEW

**Of a Way to Increase Human OKness
And Possibly Help Make the World a Better Place**

THE TRUTHER ROOSTER: A Fictionalized Story about How to Increase Human OKness in I'm OK—You're OK Adult-Adult Game-Free Dialectical Democratic Discussions, designed, marketed, and published by Inks & Bindings is a reprint of my novel *As the Rooster Crows Earthia*n *OKness Increases*, that I wrote, edited, designed, and published in 2021 using my book-publishing imprint, Effective Learning Publications.

The spinning and crowing copper rooster used in this story to randomly select leaders is a fictionalized version of a spinning device I invented in the 1970s to randomly select leaders in my case method courses at Georgia Southern University. The invention was first described in an article I published in the *Transactional Analysis Journal* in 1979, titled "The Classroom De-Gamer".

I started Effective Learning Publications in 1979 with my first self-published book *De-Gaming Teaching and Learning: How to Motivate Learners and Invite OKness* when I was 39 years old. I had 500 copies of the book printed by an offset printer and within a few years I had sold them all, mainly through TransPubs, a bookstore primarily selling books by authors with certifications and affiliations with the International Transactional Analysis Association. I had become a certified member of the ITAA with a specialization in organizations and education, not psychotherapy, in 1978 while participating in monthly weekend instruction and training sessions at the Southeast Institute at Chapel Hill, NC during 1975-78, when I was teaching as a full professor of management in the business school at Georgia Southern University, now branded as GS.

Martin Groder, MD, a psychiatrist and a leader of the TA movement in the 1970's, who studied with Eric Berne, MD, the inventor and founder of TA, was a mentor of mine at Chapel Hill. He read *De-Gaming Teaching and Learning* and made suggestions before I printed it. He called *DGTL* "A major new application of transactional analysis," and he gave me permission to quote that, which I did in my TransPub listing. His quote caused *DGTL* to sell as well as it did. I am indebted to Marty in more ways than one.

For more on my TA background and training read my articles "RJS Ancestry and Scripting" nd "RJS Athletic, Business, and Academic Vita" in my *Effective Learning Report* at <u>www.</u>

effectivelearning.net These articles are also published in my 2025 book, *Gee, You're Wonderful, Professor: How to Motivate Learners and Increase OKness with I'm OK-You're OK Adult-Adult Game-Free Dialectical Case-Based Learning Processes*, designed, published, and marketed by Genre Library Solutions.

I updated and retitled *De-Gaming Teaching and Learning* as *Born to Learn* and republished it under my Effective Learning Publications imprint in 2016, selling about 100 copies through Amazon.com. I reprinted an update of this version of *Born to Learn* in *Gee, You're Wonderful, Professor*, which is now the best buy of all my books. I also republished a new stand-alone version of *Born to Learn,* designed and marketed by Primix Publishing, in 2025.

In GYWP you get *DGTL/Born to Learn* that explains how transactional analysis concepts can be applied in formal learning processes, while defining basic TA words and terms, plus a new section called Aspirations, Applications, Ideas showing how I applied TA in cases and learning processes of all sorts up to now.

What you get with *The Truther Rooster* is a demonstration showing what might happen if you somehow started an I'm OK—You're OK Adult-Adult Game-Free Dialectical Case-Based discussion group where you live.

I invented, started, wrote, owned, and published my own news medium, The *Wolfforth-Frenship Gazette*, a weekly newspaper, when I was 22 years old during 1963-65, after earning a bachelor's degree in economics in 1962 at Texas Tech University.

I grew up in Wolfforth, a shanty town with a paved highway running through it parallel to a Santa Fe railroad track, comprising about 15 small businesses, a railroad side-car cattle loading corral and chute, three filling stations, a garage, a blacksmith shop, two grocery stores, a butane distributor, my parents' lumber yard and hardware and paint store, two cotton gins, a grain elevator, and two cafes; plus the Frenship School District grade, junior high, and high school brick buildings; three churches, a Methodist, a Baptist, and a Church of Christ; a fenced-in Lubbock County facility housing maintainers used to scrape dirt roads and clean out bar ditches that were cut in square miles in surrounding erstwhile Indian land/range land, subdivided into prosperous cotton farms irrigated with fresh water pumped from the Ogallala Aquifer; a tiny wooden building housing a public library funded by Lubbock County; a lighted Little League baseball field sponsored by the Lion's Club; a lighted arena for roping contests where would-be cowboys pranced around on their quarter horses and chased and roped calves that zoomed into the arena when released from a gated chute, acting like Medieval knights prancing around on their steeds in lists at jousting tournaments; the lighted Frenship Stadium where junior high and high school boys suffered butterflies, bruises, and exhaustion gutting it out for glory, girlfriends, and adrenalin highs fighting in football games against teams from similar towns on the South Plains of Texas.

Such was Wolfforth comprising about 200-500 residents, circa 1940-1962.

By the time I started the newspaper in 1963 Wolfforth had grown a little and had a bank, started by my father Dick Stapleton and a lawyer from Lubbock Jim Moore. Dick had also started the first housing subdivision in the town in an erstwhile cotton field, building and selling brick three-bedroom ranch style houses, financed with 20-year F.H.A. mortgage loans with monthly payments. I had also started the first real estate, fire and casualty insurance, and mortgage loan agency in the town, Rick Stapleton Agency. The Frenship School District of Lubbock County also comprised four other towns that were smaller than Wolfforth that I also covered with local news, commentary, and advertising.

Four part-time paid associates helped me put out the paper and I netted a profit from the paper, about $3000 a year, about $30,000 in 2026 money adjusted for inflation; but things did not look good to me in Wolfforth in January 1964, after being in the newspaper business about one year. I sold the paper and the new owner defaulted on his promissory note to me after about six months. I took the paper back and ran it for about six more months. When the paper had published two years of consecutive weekly issues I shut it down, sending out pro rata checks for unexpired subscriptions to subscribers.

Milton Kirksey, a cotton farmer with a degree from Texas Tech, who was on the Frenship School Board and the Frenship Co-op Association board of directors, a cotton gin owned by farmers, told me, "Aren't you a little young to be retiring?" Herb Henderson, also a cotton farmer and the manager of the grain elevator, who played basketball for a while at Texas Tech, told me, "We all can't get scared and run off," after I told him I wondered what would happen when the irrigation water played out. Irrigation wells around Wolfforth that were pumping 8-inch pipes of water in 1940 were pumping 3-inch pipes of water in 1965.

I went back to graduate school at Texas Tech about ten miles up the highway at Lubbock where I earned a master's degree in organizational behavior and a doctor's degree in management science.

The top learning producers in my case at Texas Teach were Harry Walker in the history of economic thought and H. A. Anderson in comparative economic systems at the bachelor's level; Vincent Luchsinger in organizational behavior at the master's level; and Vernon Clover in economic geography, Howard Balsley in Bayesian statistics, Carleton Whitehead in organizations, and Richard Barton in management science at the doctor's level.

When I was in graduate school I talked from time to time with a psychiatrist in his office in Lubbock, Jerome Smith, MD, telling him what I had had on my mind since the last visit and getting his feedback. I am convinced his expertise and skill helped me create a better life script outcome for me than would otherwise have been the case. For more detail on this read my article "RJS Ancestry and Scripting" in my *Effective Learning Report* at www.effectivelearning.com.

After working my way through graduate school as a management teaching assistant one year and a part-time instructor in economic history three years, I emerged in the fall of 1969 as an associate professor of management at the University of Louisiana at Lafayette, skipping the assistant professor level, with my doctor's degree in hand where I learned how the Harvard Business School Case Method worked at that time, teaching with Bernard Bienvenu and Rexford Hauser, HBS doctorates, who mandated that all courses in the management department had to be taught using the HBS case method.

I had problems adjusting and flexing to the HBS case method, or at least the version of it demonstrated by Bernard and Rex, who were great teachers, as evidenced by the quantity and quality of learning they were producing in students. I had never been around professors who had the kind of respect and rapport they had with their students. I felt inadequate by comparison. However, about halfway through my second semester there using their case process it dawned on me how it worked, my OKness level went up, and I felt successful teaching in the department.

Unfortunately by this time I had already accepted a position at another university at a higher salary; but I used nothing but the case method for the rest of my teaching career, making me a lone wolf and a pariah of sorts at one point at Georgia Southern University, after I left UL-Lafayette after one academic year, becoming the only professor using the case method in the business school at GS. I am the only professor I know of who adopted and used a teaching method throughout his career that was not scripted and learned by osmosis observing and copying the teaching methods his/her favorite teachers used during long years of formal schooling as a student sitting in their classrooms.

Scripted teachers in my opinion rarely change their teaching scripts throughout their careers, including their teaching methods, classroom layouts, and testing and grading procedures. Paul LaGrone, the GS business dean that recruited me to GS in 1970, in about 1992 told me in a golf cart as we were drinking beer while playing in the annual GS School of Business golf tournament that, "Everything would have been fine if you just hadn't used those *damn* circles!"

I used circle classroom layouts requiring students to reposition row and column layout desks around the perimeters of classrooms and put them back like they were at the end of class. It was obvious to me that quite a few professors, administrators, and students were bothered by this; but no one told me point blank that I could not do it, so I kept doing it, being convinced it was causing my students to learn and increase OKness more than they otherwise would have.

While at UL-Lafayette in academic year 1969-70, I also learned about transactional analysis after reading *Games People Play* and *What Do You Do After You Say Hello,* by Eric Berne, MD, a psychiatrist, which I received through the Book of the Month Club. These learning experiences caused me to evolve my I'm OK–You're OK Adult-Adult Game-Free dialectical case-based Learning process that I used up to my retirement as the Senior Professor at GS in 2005, having joined GS in June 1970 as the highest paid professor in the university.

My book-publishing venture Effective Learning Publications has been more of a philanthropy than a business. Counting seminars and other paid consulting resulting from selling 500 copies of *De–Gaming Teaching and Learning* the book project netted a profit. However, none of my Effective Learning Publications POD (Print on Demand) books have generated enough revenue to cover their costs of production and marketing, with the possible exception of *Born to Learn.*

Regardless, it may be the illusion of selling thousands of well-crafted POD books with compelling covers and well-laid-out interiors at Amazon.com and in bookstores everywhere plus the overall creative process of writing and publishing books has been worth it, in psychic income, giving me something to do that might have made a difference after retiring as a professor, given the banality and boredom of most other time-structuring alternatives.

It's amazing to me that anyone can make a decent living writing and selling books anymore. I read on the Internet recently that Amazon.com publishes, or at least lists for sale, over one million new books per year. This is hard to believe, but there is no doubt that the Internet has increased competition in the information business by several orders of magnitude.

The Internet has given anyone a theoretical chance to say and teach whatever they want to someone or anyone anywhere; but Internet algorithms have also herded conformist might-have-been-book-reading Earthian humans into isolated polarized wormholes of avarice, malice, and misinformation, shut off from relevant outside information. Seems to me the Internet may have reduced the probability of ordinary humans teaching or learning anything about scripted human states of affairs around Spaceship Earth to or from anyone outside their scripted families and support groups, thereby reducing the probability of comprehensive consensual learning happening among ordinary humans all around Spaceship Earth, leaving ordinary humans everywhere as divided and conquered as ever by greedy brutish power-mad Game infested leaders, vulnerable to vicissitudes of all sorts.

Scripted Red states and countries tend to stay red, and scripted Blue states and countries tend to stay blue, loathing and fighting one another, with scripted ordinary humans obeying their leaders, generation after generation; and very likely they will continue acting out their scripts—till the cows come home—unless new efficient and effective learning processes are innovated or evolved and are somehow implemented all around Spaceship Earth.

My fictionalized story *The Truther Rooster* is an attempt to ameliorate this pernicious dumbing-down anti-intellectual side effect of the Internet by paying forty randomly-selected characters from all regions and walks of life of the US $5,000 per month to attend monthly weekend sessions of a seminar in downtown hotels of randomly-selected cities of the US to discuss problems and opportunities facing humans all around Spaceship Earth, in an I'm OK-You're OK Adult-Adult Game-Free dialectical fully-democratic free-thinking bottom-up case-based learning process.

Seems to me $5,000 a month might be enough to entice most humans from all walks of life in the US to get out of their wormholes once a month on a weekend to participate in a seminar such as this one, to help create comprehensive consensual bottom-up policies and strategies for rationally dealing with existential threats.

Every new discussion episode of the Truther Rooster seminar is started by spinning a copper rooster in the center of a circle learning layout, who raucously crows and vigorously bobs his head up and down when spun, to let all the characters around the room know it's time to wake up and get to work.

If you are selected as the "Leader of the Moment" to start the discussion by The Truther Rooster you have to answer in your opening remarks three Adult ego state questions:

What is the problem or opportunity?

What are the alternatives?

What do you recommend?

You have to tell the group what you truthfully and honestly think is the most relevant problem or opportunity facing Earthian humans right now, however naive, uninformed, dumb, intelligent, cogent, or wise your analysis might be. If you don't you can be fined or fired by Rout Logger.

When the Leader of the Moment finishes her/his opening spiel other characters can then dive in the dialectical process on a first come-first serve basis to correct or buttress the leader's answers by agreeing or disagreeing with relevant or irrelevant points and analyses the Leader of the Moment brought up. There can be no holding up of hands to break the natural line-up of the first come-first serve queue. When the arguing loses steam and winds down and the discussants have generated some good consensual answers about what to do about the case the Leader of the Moment brought up The Truther Rooster is spun again, by the previous leader of the moment, to select a new Leader of the Moment, and so it goes month after month, gradually increasing the OKness of the characters by changing their scripting in various ways, caused by the relentless barrage of dialectical dialogical counter-arguments and supporting embellishments, causing the characters to feel, think, comprehend, and do better than they had been, i.e., increasing their OKness.

If only the US and all other countries around Spaceship Earth could change Leaders of the Moment and generate good consensual answers about what to do about relevant problems and opportunities in cases while increasing human OKness this efficiently and effectively the world would indeed become a much better place.

I'm OK—You're OK Adult-Adult Game-Free Dialectical Democratic learning processes such as this one in this book if widely adopted would not be a cure-all for solving all the world's problems; but they would be better than allowing scripted Not-OK power-mad fascist Game-infested leaders to make the world pay, commit genocides, and kill Earthian humans in wars, applying and propagating scripted I'm OK—We're OK—You're Not OK life positions and loser life scripts, using Parent-Child transactions, and playing third degree tissue-tearing psychological Games such as NIGYSOB, Now I've Got You, You SOB and IF IT WEREN'T FOR YOU, trying to prove what big-shots they are, trying to be superior and reign supreme.

A sobering finding and teaching of transactional analysis is that Earthian humans are scripted before the age of eight or so with psychological and social messages that are powerful enough to cause them to turn out as they do in the end, producing in a state of nature three generic life outcomes: winner, banal, and loser. Life scripts can be changed by various forms of psychotherapy, but the vast majority of Earthian humans cannot afford or access good psychotherapy services and treatments, which is unfair, caused by concatenations of infinitely regressive and progressive cause-effect chains causing the scripting to happen.

A problem in ordinary discussions and governmental deliberations and conversations around Spaceship Earth is that discussants cannot use Adult-Adult transactions. They have been forced to use Parent-Parent, Parent-Child, and Child-Child transactions in discussions, engaging in small talk that does not help anyone comprehend or consider what is really going on in social and psychological states of affairs around Spaceship Earth. It's considered rude or arrogant for Earthian humans to cathect Adult ego states to start Adult-Adult transactions in ordinary conversations by talking about any of the three Adult ego state questions listed above, thereby conserving the existing probability that ordinary humans will conserve their existing OKness levels and sources of satisfaction in their wormholes, thereby conserving the low probability that any sort of progress in human states of affairs will happen, exacerbating existing polarizations of progressives and conservatives, winners and loser-survivors, and poor and rich everywhere.

Cathect in this context means to turn on or energize an ego state. The Truther Rooster process forces the Leader of the Moment to cathect an Adult ego state to start a case discussion. Most of the characters had difficulties adapting their group imagoes and flexing their personalities enough to feel comfortable participating in the learning process at the beginning, but most of them had adapted and flexed enough by the end of the seminar to feel OK participating in the group.

Parent, Adult, and Child ego states are manifested by looks, mannerisms, gestures, body posture, voice tone, volume and speed of talking, word choices, phrases, glares, stares, smiles, smirks, raising or lowering of eyebrows and eyelids, focusing or squinting of eyes, jutting out of chins, clamping of jaw muscles, tightening or relaxing of facial muscles, pointing with index fingers, squaring or slumping of shoulders, indicating feelings, thoughts, and behaviors that are parent-like, adult-like, and child-like. Eric Berne liked to play poker considering poker to be an Adult ego state game that tested transactional analysis skills. In order to know what is really going on you have to know what is really going on with those with whom you are transacting; and body language signals can help you bet to win rather than lose. Berne was convinced those who win more than they lose playing poker win because of skill at seeing what is really going on around the table, not getting lucky.

Like Don Quixote, here I go again, at age 85, jousting one more windmill, with one more book, my most grandiose illusion of all, saving the world by rolling out zoom technology seminar copies of my I'm OK-You're OK Adult-Adult Game-Free Dialectical Case-Based Democratic free-thinking bottom-up management seminar all around Spaceship Earth, featuring the fictional would-be hero Rout Logger and the Truther Rooster conducting a series of monthly weekend seminar sessions to eradicate the probability of global warming and climate change (GWCC) and militarization and nuclear weapons proliferation (MNWP) causing the extinction of Earthian humans.

The danger of religions, especially those that emphasize the existence of an old man living eternally up in the sky who has enough knowledge, intelligence, and power to create all humans in the world, and take care of them eternally, if only they love him and obey his commands, is that they tend to generate I'm OK—We're OK, but they are Not OK life positions, Parent and Child transactions, and the playing of psychological Games by Persecutors, Victims, and Rescuers on Drama Triangles, Games such as NIGYSOB, DO ME SOMETHING, I'M ONLY TRYING TO HELP YOU, AIN'T IT AWFUL, and GREENHOUSE. The major problem in the US right now (March 30, 2026) is that the supreme leader of the US has started a war with Iran and some of his military leaders are telling their troops that they are fighting in a holy war. While this sort of thing may create feelings of patriotism and holy zeal and grandeur it is also nihilistic, valuing violence, destruction, suffering, and death. While some of these religious sects claim to especially value human life itself, and their life position is pro-life for Earthian humans who were scripted with religious beliefs such as theirs; their life position for scripted others may be pro-death. Some of these sects try to produce as many children as possible, and even attempt to restrict birth control and outlaw abortions for everyone, which they consider pro-life; but unfortunately this life position strategy leads to producing an overpopulation of humans in a country, that leads to increasing poverty in a country, that leads to the creation of authoritarian leaders and authoritarian social, economic, political, and religious systems, that lead to stealing from other countries to survive, that leads to violence and wars, that leads to unnatural deaths, becoming by no means pro-life in the end.

Eric Berne said all humans are born princes and princesses until their parents turn them into frogs. Parents who were scripted with winner, banal, and loser scripts automatically as if by osmosis in turn script their offspring socially and psychologically with the same scripts, and so it goes generation after generation until *force majeure* events force change in family scripts, or lucky individuals change their loser and banal scripts into better ones through psychotherapy in relatively-free countries.

Unfortunately one way naturally-occurring individual scripts can be changed is for dictators to impose draconian fascist authoritarian economic and political systems on almost everyone in the country in which leaders create new scripts that all followers in the country have to act out, in which almost all humans in the country are ruled by regime leaders somewhat like military personnel are ruled in armies and the like by officers and military codes. Quite a few countries around Spaceship Earth now fit this mold in various degrees, China, North Korea, Russia, Iran, Saudi Arabia, to name a few. Donald Trump, the now supreme leader of the US, wants to do somewhat the same in the US. All businesses script their workers in this fashion to some degree for eight or so hours per day in supposedly free countries.

Back in the 1970s I thought membership in the International Transactional Analysis Association would continue to increase indefinitely. Membership in the association grew in the 1960s and 1970s from zero to about 10,000 members; but things changed around 1980 in the US. Along came Reaganomics with its trickle-down absurdity—the fantasy that everyone can get rich by making the already rich richer by cutting their taxes and by cutting government expenses for social programs, while increasing military expenses, and, adding insult to injury, by out-sourcing high-wage blue-collar jobs to low-wage countries, not to mention using AI robots to do the jobs of human workers, which, according to the

Republican life position and strategy, would magically result in so much economic growth in the US that even the poor would get richer.

Well, this was a complete farce. The rich got richer alright, while the poor stayed the same or got poorer, resulting in the creation of many millions of loser-survivors who were left behind with marginal precarious incomes and diminished social status in the private sector of the US.

The Republican conservative movement grew and ITAA membership shrank from about 10,000 to less than 1,000. The conservative Republican movement in the US inexorably wound up creating about 77 million loser survivors who voted for Donald Trump again in 2024, exacerbating the sad social, economic, and political state of affairs now existing in the US and worldwide. TA and other personal growth movements withered on the vine. This did not happen because TA did not "work" for users. The problem was that most of those who used TA and benefitted from it did not renew their memberships in the TA association, the ITAA, after they got as OK as they wanted to be and fewer and fewer new users wanted to learn about TA. The problem is that no one can be fully OK if all humans are not somewhat OK, and for all humans to be somewhat OK social, economic, and political systems have got to be somewhat OK. Few Earthian humans want to work for increased personal OKness when they are threatened by social, economic, and political problems, and, unfortunately, in order for TA to work, individuals using TA have to work to make changes. Merely believing or pretending to believe something someone tells you will not increase your OKness, and nor will voting for, financially supporting, or obeying fascist leaders playing I'M ONLY TRYING TO HELP YOU.

If Earthian humans cannot somehow create OK social, economic, and political systems humans may become extinct around Spaceship Earth.

In the meantime, the main thing Trump's 77 million loser-survivor voters have to worry about is Trump successfully doing what he has said he wants to do, i.e., turn the US into an authoritarian fascist dictatorship with himself installed as dictator for the rest of his life, in which case, if it happens, his voters will not be rewarded with a MAGA utopia. Instead they will be ruled like the workers of China, North Korea, Russia, and other authoritarian dictatorships. Unfortunately, if this should happen, millions of current USian winner-survivors will be pulled down to the same level, and many will be disappeared.

For whatever it's worth, I published peer-reviewed quantitative research data in *Gee, You're Wonderful, Professor* showing my learning process used in the business school at GS motivated learners in my courses to study more than students choosing alternative processes used in the department, causing me to rank 1 of 29 in the department in study production. I was not a wonderful professor in terms of instructor excellence, ranking 24 of 29. On the other hand, based on a ranking of a composite score derived from an equal weighting of instructor excellence, study production, learning production, and expected grades production scores I ranked 5 of 29. These data were published in "Optimizing the Fairness of Student Evaluations: A Study of Correlations Between Instructor Excellence, Study Production, Learning Production, and Expected Grades," by Stapleton & Murkison, published in the *Journal of Management Education* in 2001, listed in the References section of this book, reprinted in full in *Gee, You're Wonderful, Professor.* For a quick summary of the article showing citations, references, and data punch "Optimizing the Fairness of Student Evaluations" into Google and click on Semantic Scholar.

I also included in *Gee, You're Wonderful, Professor* longitudinal data from another research project Gene Murkison and I conducted showing learners choosing my Adult-Adult case-based process for two or more courses, five to fifteen years after graduating at GS, reported earning higher incomes than students in the management department who avoided my courses, who took the same courses taught by professors using Parent-Child ego states and transactions, authoritarian lectures, row and column layouts, and standard testing and grading methods.

I am the only professor or teacher of any kind I know of who produced in his career longitudinal data indicating his learning process worked better for students in their careers than alternative learning processes used by teachers teaching the same courses to students drawn from the same pool of students.

The strongest correlation of all in this longitudinal study was a .245 Pearson's r correlation between number of I'm OK-You're OK Adult-Adult Game-Free dialectical democratic case-based courses taken and reported incomes. Some learners chose five or more of my courses, and they reported the highest incomes of all. The respondents were asked to list four professors from whom they thought they learned the most. I was listed 52 times, one professor was listed 51 times, and several others were listed from 20-30 times. Asked what they would recommend for improving the GS business school they overwhelmingly recommended more case method courses. Respondents were guaranteed anonymity and Gene Murkison, who did not use the case method, signed the cover letter for the questionnaire mailout.

Some of these data were published in an article my wife Debbye and I published in the *Transactional Analysis Journal* in 1998, Stapleton & Stapleton, "Teaching Business Using the Case Method and Transactional Analysis: A Constructivist Approach," also listed in the references of this book. Deborah Coleman Stapleton is an emeritus assistant professor of mathematics at GS.

I am convinced learning processes such as the one demonstrated by Rout Logger in *The Truther Rooster* would increase human OKness all around Spaceship Earth, however uncomfortable most Earthian humans would be when first exposed to it. While the supposedly randomly-selected characters in this book are fictional I have heard responses and arguments similar to those the characters used made by real learners in my courses, seminars, and group discussions in various organizations and groups in several countries, as shown in my RJS Athletic, Business, and Academic Vita, published in my *Effective Learning Report* at <u>www.effectivelearning.net</u> .

Gee, You're Wonderful, Professor is the name of a psychological Game, one of the most ubiquitous Games played in schools, colleges, and universities, and in learning processes of all sorts everywhere, that I tried not to play. This Game is a cause or concomitant of passivity, grade inflation, and other dishonesties and dysfunctions in learning processes everywhere. GYWP is a softer version of a psychological Game called PEASANT.

For more on transactional analysis in general or psychological Games in particular just punch words into Google or any Internet search engine … such as … Information on transactional analysis … or … Eric Berne and Gee, You're Wonderful, Professor at YouTube. You can pull up more information on the subject than you have ever dreamt of.

Here's my definition of transactional analysis: An art and science for increasing human OKness taking into account ego states, transactions, scripts, Games, life positions, time structuring alternatives, and contracts to comprehend, predict, and change human behavior using stacked P-A-C ego state circle diagrams.

I have defined and visually demonstrated these TA words, concepts, and circles in *Born to Learn*. They are demonstrated verbally in dialogues in this book *The Truther Rooster*.

Born to Learn is reprinted in *Gee, You're Wonderful, Professor* along with a new section called Aspirations, Applications, Ideas showing how I applied TA in hundreds of cases in several countries through the years, mostly in the US, providing evidence I increased Earthian human OKness to some extent at some points, possibly not causing any lasting noticeable effects, but at least taking steps in a positive direction creating temporary OKness increases.

The genius of TA, invented by Eric Berne, MD, in the 1960s, is that it created an easy-to-learn language comprising ordinary words, terms, and symbols that enabled ordinary Earthian humans all around Spaceship Earth to understand what is really going on in complex social and psychological states of affairs better than they otherwise would have.

This book featuring Rout Logger and the Truther Rooster demonstrates what might happen if you somehow started an

I'm OK—You're OK Adult-Adult Game-Free Dialectical Case-Based discussion group where you live.

The learning process in this book is Game-Free because Rout Logger and the Classroom De-Gamer™, aka The Truther Rooster, banished Karpman Drama Triangles of Persecutors, Victims, and Rescuers from the Discussion Room.

If every home, church, school house, business, and government building around Spaceship Earth had such a room....

Best wishes,
Richard John Stapleton
Cedar Hill
University Park
Bulloch County
Georgia
United States of America
March 30, 2026

1

HOW IT GOT STARTED

Henry thought it was junk mail. Why would anyone want to pay him five thousand dollars a day to participate in some sort of discussion group?

He deleted the message thinking it was a scam of some sort—but the email messages kept coming.

He replied to the sender and told him to take him off the list and threatened to notify the police, but the sender assured him the offer was real and legal, and to prove it a bank account had been set up in his name with an initial deposit of one hundred dollars, which he could verify with a username and password, which turned out to be true. Henry withdrew fifty dollars from the account using an ATM machine.

He thought he must be insane to even dream about getting involved with a screwball idea like this. There was no telling what kind of outfit was behind it, and there had to be a catch somewhere. Why would anyone pay him to show up at a hotel and talk with people? How had they found him? What did they know about him?

He finally emailed the anonymous sender telling him or her there was an account in his name and he had withdrawn fifty dollars. He asked the sender to send him the name and address of the organization responsible for this. He said he wanted proof the offer was legal.

He received an email informing him the group financing the project was ethical and legal, ethics being one of their major purposes, the ultimate objectives of the project being to foster free, fair, ethical, legal and progressive behavior around Earth that would contribute to the survival of as many plant and animal species as possible, including *homo sapiens*, and there was no question about the legality of the project. The email said Henry should attend the first meeting of the group and discuss these issues with people at the meeting, the first meeting having been scheduled in the Brown Hotel in Louisville, Kentucky on the first Saturday of the coming October.

The e-mailer said his name was Dr. Rout Logger. All meetings would be held in hotels in different cities the first Saturday of each month until such time as the sponsors decided to terminate the program. The sponsors were citizens concerned about preserving life on Earth. All participants would be paid five thousand dollars per Saturday meeting, deposited monthly in their bank accounts established by the sponsor. Participants would be responsible for arranging their own transportation to and from the meetings with food and lodging to be paid from their monthly fee. They could stay and eat wherever they chose in the various cities.

Logger wrote in the email that group members would meet in formal sessions in designated, secure meeting rooms, which would be protected by a private security service. Group sessions would be conducted from nine a.m. to noon and from two p.m. to five p.m. on the first Saturday of each month. If Henry replied to this email agreeing to attend the November meeting, five thousand dollars would be deposited in his bank account. On Mondays following Saturday meetings attended another five thousand would be deposited in his account for the next meeting. It was permissible to miss a monthly meeting for compelling reasons, but after missing a monthly meeting no additional deposits would be made until after attendance at the next meeting. The city and hotel selected for the next month would be announced in emails sent the Monday following the last meeting.

Participants could discuss whatever they wanted to discuss. Logger said each session would be started by randomly selecting the group leader, by spinning a colorful copper rooster in the center of the meeting room about three feet tall that crowed when spun. Whomever the spinning crowing rooster stopped on would answer three questions:

What is the Problem?
What are the Alternatives?
What do you Recommend?

The meetings were to be conducted in rooms large enough to accommodate forty participants, who would use their first names in the group, aliases being permissible. There would be no breaks during the three-hour sessions but participants would be excused for legitimate calls of nature. No eating or drinking would occur during the sessions. There would be no physical touching or psychological transactions during group meetings.

The group members had been randomly selected using various criteria and processes to form a group of disparate humans of various ages, races, sexes, genders, sexual orientations, socio-economic levels, and intelligence levels from all walks of life believing diverse beliefs.

All sessions would be audio and video-recorded. Some of the information collected would eventually be published in reports making recommendations for sustaining Earthian human life, made available to all humans aboard Spaceship Earth.

It bothered Henry that this guy did not tell him the name of the sponsoring group or organization, but he decided to go to at least one meeting. What were the chances you might get shot, tortured, kidnapped or something? Pretty slim he thought. If you got paid five thousand dollars for doing nothing but talk it was worth taking a chance. But where did this Earthian crap come from?

2

HOW IT HAPPENED

**SESSION ONE
LOUISVILLE, KENTUCKY
OCTOBER 2019**

The hotel conference room was a large square room furnished with comfortable armchairs arranged in a circle that left enough space between the circle and the walls for someone to walk around the outerperimeter of the circle.

A large colorful copper rooster resembling a weather vane stood in the center of the room on a round wooden base. An iron rod about four feet longextending from a base held the rooster erect in sucha way that it would spin when twirled. The rooster was programmed to bob its head up and down and raucously crow when someone gave him a spin. Whoever was in a line of imaginary fire extending from the rooster's head to her or him sitting in the circle when he stopped spinning would become the Leader of the Moment.

About twenty people were present. Henry sat in the nearest empty chair, making eye contact with two or three people nearby. It was ten minutes before nine o'clock.

The armchairs had almost filled up by nine a.m., at which time Rout Logger briskly walked into the room, carrying a large leather briefcase, seating himself in one of the empty armchairs, which were identical.

"Good morning folks. I'm Rout Logger. It's good to see you. I'm glad you could make it. Hopefully we'll be seeing more of one another in these meetings for a good while. Thanks for being here. I see a few members are not here yet, but we'll get started anyway. Please make sure you are on time from now on. It's rude, disrespectful, and disruptive for anyone to come in late.

"I think most of you generally understand the purpose of the meetings, the times for the meetings and so forth. You were all sent the same emails introducing the process. Here's the procedure we'll be using in the sessions. We want the discussions to be honest, full, and frank. We'll start every discussion by spinning that rooster out there in the center of the room, called The Truther. I'll spin it the first time myself to kick off the process; from then on whoever got pointed out last spins it next. The purpose of spinning The Truther is to randomly select the leader of a discussion, guaranteeing each member has an equal chance to be the leader of every session, excluding the person making the spin. The last person hit by the Truther rooster will spin it next. If The Truther rooster stops on me I'll serve as the leader myself, just as any of you would if it landed on you. We want to foster equality among members and response-able, efficient, effective, intelligent, critical, and creative feeling, thinking, and behaving in the group. While I am the formal leader of the group I have as much right as anyone else to be the designated leader of the day, if selected by The Truther.

"I originated the idea for The Truther and this project and secured the funding. Most of the donors are wealthy individuals. The donors shall remain anonymous, but I can tell you they have donated funds for this project based on their hope the process might contribute to improving the quality of life, and chances of survival, of all species of fauna and flora around Spaceship Earth.

"The donors are convinced if *homo sapiens* on Earth do not make significant changes in their feeling, thinking, believing, and behaving patterns dire consequences will result, possibly resulting in the extinction of the human species sooner than later. If it can be demonstrated that this process produced increased OKness in this group hopefully similar groups will be established around Spaceship Earth. Each of you is being paid the same for your attendance and participation, five thousand dollars for each monthly session in which you participate. Do the math. Since there are forty of you in the group this amounts to almost two and one half million dollars per year for group member compensation, about three and one-half million per year for total expenses, counting my salary, logistics, room reservations, support staff, security, computers, furniture, and what have you.

"I have an undergraduate degree in economics, a master's degree in organizational behavior, and a PhD in management science that entailed empirical, mathematical, and computer-based training, plus I have had post-doctoral training in psychological techniques, including a certification in transactional analysis. I have experience in athletics; entrepreneurship; teaching and research; management consulting and training; and research, writing, and publishing dealing with operations management, organizational analysis, policy formulation, manpower motivation and productivity, and organizational development for universities and various kinds of organizations and groups.

"My job here is not to impart information *per se* but to facilitate the creation of new comprehension of the Earthian plight to generate recommendations for changes. Everything you say in these group discussions will be recorded and videotaped and any information generated may be used in a summary report for improving Earthian states of affairs. You will be able to access anything I have said or anything any one of you has said in these meetings using your computer in the meeting room, but you may not copy, save, forward, or share the information. None of you will be personally identified in the report. Anything you say, however, may be quoted in the report, attributed to the first name you choose to use in the group. The report may be published anywhere around Spaceship Earth. This process won't work if two or more of you use the same first name. As we go around the room, if someone has already announced your desired first name, use a first name no one has already announced; aliases are fine.

"OK, let's go around the room, proceeding clockwise, with this gentleman to my immediate left. Just give the name you want to be known by in the group and say something about what you do."

"Hello everyone, I'm John. I'm a systems engineer and programmer.

"My name is Wendel. I'm a farmer."

"I'm Ellie, a teacher."

"I'm Helen. I'm a nurse."

"Hi, I go by Hal. I'm an attorney."

"My friends call me Joan. I'm a supervisor with an insurance company."

"Bud. I'm a mechanical engineer."

"My name is Maria, a social worker."

"Bob. I'm a physician."

"Sam. Writer and social activist."
"Napoleon. Retired military."
"Margaret. I work for the government."
"Luke. Retired minister."
"George. Politician, state senator."
"Julia. I run a cleaning service."
"Henry. I own my own business. Construction."
"Bubba. I'm a farmer."
"Bill. Educator."
"Tony. A bartender."
"Mikhail. An accountant."
"Judy. Housewife and mother."
"Matilda. Librarian.
"Joe, the plumber."
"Harrison. Corporate CEO."
"Stuart. College student."
"Dick. US representative."
"Nancy. I own my own beauty shop."
"Rupert. I'm a banker."
"Clarence. Lawyer."
"Albert. University professor. Physics."
"Barbara. I'm a housewife."
"Ron. Truck driver."
"Marshall. Weatherman."
"Jimmy. Labor union organizer."
"Steve. I work in our family manufacturing business."

"Marian. Elementary teacher."

"Horatio. I own some small businesses."

"Martin. University professor, religious studies."

"Trudy. I'm a psychotherapist."

"Dan. I'm an insurance agent."

"Adam. Economics professor."

"Socrates. University professor, philosophy."

"Ellen. I just graduated from college. Looking for a job. Can't believe I was given five thousand dollars to attend this six-hour seminar."

"Andy. I'm a cop."

"Joel. I'm an economist and a social activist."

Dr. Logger got up, walked to the center of the room, and twirled The Truther rooster. The roostercrowed bobbing its head up and down to let the group members know it was time to wake up and get to work. As The Truther spun round and round,winding down, Logger said, "If it stops on you, just tell us what you think is the problem, what are the alternatives, and what you recommend."

The group members were shocked and aghast.

Bubba jerked upright in his chair as if he had been struck by lightning after the raucously crowing Truther rooster, head bobbing up and down, spinning round and round, finally stopped, pointing right at him, like a bird dog on the scent.

Glaring at Rout, a bewildered Bubba said, "You mean you want me to tell these people about some problem? What do you mean, a problem? What problem?"

Rout—"Whatever you think the most relevant problem is right now."

Bubba—"You mean what I think is the most relevant problem in the whole damn world?"

R—"Basically, yes."

B—"How would I know?"

R—"If you did know, what would it be? What's the first thing that pops up in your mind?"

B—"Well, I guess, jobs."

R—"Why is that a problem?"

B—"Why, hell, any damn fool knows it's a problem when you have people goin' hungry, folks can't find jobs."

R—"Good, that's a start. What are the alternatives?"

B—"I don't have the foggiest idea."

R—"Yes, you do."

B—"Well, I guess we could make sure people can find work or somethin'."

R—"How would you do that?"

B—"Beats the hell out of me."

R—"No recommendations at all?"

B—"Nope."

Dr. Logger thanked Bubba for kicking the process off and told the group once a discussion had been opened and the randomly-selected leader stopped talking the group would then discuss what had been said on a free-flow basis until the problems and issues brought up by the randomly selected leader had been exhausted of discussable points, discussable points being relevant points in the opinion of group members. He said one of the major tasks in these discussions was to identify relevant points from the mass of possible points, most of which were irrelevant. Once the relevant points were separated from the irrelevant points the task became to see how the relevant points related to one another to comprehend the problem well enough to make recommendations having a decent probability of producing a beneficial outcome.

He told them when the randomly-selected leader finished his or her opening remarks others should then join in on a first-come first-serve basis, meaning the first person to speak up then had the floor until s/he said what was on her or his mind about the problem, the alternatives, and the recommendations. He said quite naturally disagreements will result, and arguing about various points is a vital and necessary part of the process, necessary to separate irrelevant focal point entities from the relevant. He said it was the responsibility of every group member to attempt to correct and educate all group members about points or focal point entities they advocated or those considered wrong said by others, trying to set dissenters and antagonists and the group straight in the process. He said unlearning what was wrong was as important as learning what was right. He said this was the only way to separate the irrelevant from the relevant.

On the other hand, Logger told them in most cases economic, political, social, and psychological problems did not have "right" answers that could be proved right, and therefore the best that could be hoped for in most cases would be for humans to develop consensual answers that would produce sustainability and satisfaction for all species around Spaceship Earth.

He said the process was roughly analogous to the naturally occurring process aboard Spaceship Earth causing the evolution of ideas and practices over time, causing beliefs, policies, and practices to happen that were acceptable in the short run but which might now be obsolete and irrelevant. In this process in this room everyone had an equal opportunity to be the Leader of the Moment to correct obsolete or irrelevant beliefs, policies, and practices anyone in the group might be carrying around in his or her head, caused by the spinning of The Truther.

He said they were not searching for absolute truth here, which could not be found, or which could not be proved right if found, but rather they wanted to generate workable propositions having decent probabilities of being considered true in the minds of most humans that would cause salutary outcomes. The best they could hope for was to find the truest of the relatively true.

Rout said there was one law for this process that must not be violated except in the case of emergencies: No one could talk when someone else was talking to the whole group, and talking to the whole group is the only kind of talking allowed.

Rout—"There can be no gossiping, commenting, or communicating of any sort—verbally or non- verbally—with members sitting to your right or left in the circle when someone is talking to the whole group. There can be no rolling of eyes, smirking, frowning, gritting of teeth, or any other non- verbal psychological communication gesture when someone is talking to the whole group. There can be no actions, social or psychological, intended to alter or influence what speakers are saying as they say it, or cause them to stop saying what they are saying, as they say it. On the other hand, you may confront them socially with counter-arguments by saying whatever you wish in an Adult manner as soon as they finish saying their piece, assuming no other member beats you to the punch by commencing to talk before you can, in an attempt to change their minds or behavior.

"After the current speaker decides to stop saying what s/he is saying, the first person to dive into the conversation then owns the floor until she or he decides to stop talking, her/his speech also being protected as was the speaking of the previous speaker; and so it goes for the duration of the process.

"If I decide to spin The Truther to select another leader, there can be no communicating of any sort, socially or psychologically, before, while, or after The Truther is spinning, except by the member randomly selected as leader of the moment by The Truther.

"The overriding law here is there can be no communicating of any sort when the process is in session except when talking to the whole group or to a specific person in response to something the person had said to the whole group, which must be said in such a way the entire group can hear everything being said. But as soon as the person owning the floor finishes talking its first-come first- serve, with the first person to start talking now owning the floor until s/he finishes communicating.

"In other words, there can be no covert, ulterior psychological communication, side deals, subversive power alliances, psychological threats, bullying or quid pro quo cronyism throughout the process at any time, however long the process shall be conducted, perhaps months, perhaps years, depending on what happens. Everything must be above board with all cards played face up on the table.

"There can be no holding up of hands to get permission to talk. You must compete with all members as an equal on a first-come first-serve basis by diving in first as soon as the person speaking stops.

"Some of you will naturally acquire larger market shares than others as the process unfolds in the free market. Peer ratings will be used from time to time to give everyone feedback regarding his/her market share. Different market shares will naturally happen due to some of you having training and knowledge especially relevant to various focal point entities that shall emerge, some of you are just naturally better communicators than others, some of you have more functional personalities than others, some of you are just naturally more intelligent and creative than others, some of you are better than others making analogous comparisons, seeing interrelations among focal point entities, and being able to comprehend whole systems. A market share in this context is your percent of the total ideas sold in the group, computed by estimating the number of ideas you sold and dividing by all ideas sold by everyone in the group. Making a sale is getting group members to agree with a new idea.

"Buckminster Fuller asserted in his *Operating Manual for Spaceship Earth* back in the 1960s that humans should comprehend whole systems, not just the parts, and the way to do this is by separating irrelevant observations from relevant focal point entities, and then comprehending how the relevant focal point entities relate to one another, where the more relevant entities there are in a system the greater the comprehension required and produced.

"Fuller defined Comprehension as a mathematical function of the number of relevant focal point entities in a system, where Comprehension = $(N^2-N)/2$ where N equals the number of relevant focal point entities in the system under consideration.

"In this process, the ultimate relevant focal system is Spaceship Earth.

"You will improve your Comprehension abilities through practice over time in this process. On the other hand, not all market shares will be equal. Each of you will have an equal opportunity to earn and accrue strokes for identifying relevant focal point entities and explaining how they interrelate, but as in any free enterprise system qualities such as ambition, courage, hard work, determination, risk-taking, and ability to endure failure are relevant in this process. Some of you shall accumulate higher stroke incomes and develop larger stroke bank accounts than others. On the other hand, all of you will be paid the same in money terms, five thousand dollars per monthly session. Since all of you inherited your abilities, knowledge, and skills by accident you are not to be blamed, praised, or monetarily rewarded for merely possessing relatively different abilities, knowledge bases, and skills, for better or worse.

"If you have a low market share don't worry about it; as with all eventualities it just accidentally or inevitably happened, given that free will most likely does not exist and all events have causes, including events such as feelings, thoughts, wishes, decisions, desires, goals and wants happening in human brains, resulting from infinitely regressive unbroken cause-effect chains going back to the beginning of time, assuming there was a beginning of time.

"Although a major objective of the process is to cause the creation of beliefs, propositions, policies, and practices that will make Earthian life fairer, more satisfying, and more sustainable, there is no way to make the prior acquisition of knowledge, skills, and ability in the group equal and fair among members. We all have our own genes, scripts, karmas and dharmas that we inherited. There is very little you or I or anyone can do right now about the cause-effect sequences that caused our brains to be programmed from birth as they are. If I were to try to make the process fair by attempting to manipulate equal market shares and stroke incomes for each of you, by requiring you to hold up hands to get my permission to speak, or by going around the room in sequence to make sure everyone has the same airtime, the creative potential of the process would be significantly diminished.

"Your *karma* is the particular sequence of cause-effect events causing you and your reality to happen to you; your *dharma* is your way of life caused by your karma.

"On the other hand, a major purpose of this process is to cause over time the natural inevitable and accidental cause-effect chain causing you to be who and what you are right now to be changed in such a way as to cause you to accept consensual answers caused to be developed in this process that could cause all species aboard Spaceship Earth to experience satisfying and sustainable lives.

"That's a tall order I know; but that's what we're up to, however improbable it is it will be achieved.

"One develops market share by selling ideas to the group about the problem or opportunity under consideration, that become relevant focal point entities. Selling an idea means others think you are right, regardless of whether you really are. Trying to sell irrelevant ideas in most cases will not produce sales and market shares or cause you to receive high-quality positive strokes. A stroke is a unit of recognition. On the other hand, you will receive and aggregate more strokes by trying to sell irrelevant observations than by not trying. The only way you can know whether your observations and ideas are relevant is by trying to sell them.

"The USian comedian W.C. Fields was incorrect when he said, 'Tis far better to remain silent, and be thought a fool, than to speak up and remove all doubt.'

"It's possible The Truther rooster will never select you as a Leader of the Moment in this process, thereby not guaranteeing you get some strokes, either positive or negative. You must volunteer observations, ideas, and the like to ensure that you get some strokes, competing on a first-come first-serve basis with all group members after the group member owning the floor finishes saying whatever s/he wants to say.

"Most *homo sapiens* have a strong need to be recognized for their achievements, and receiving positive strokes are among their greatest satisfactions. Satisfaction is the most common human goal. Some forms of satisfaction may result in deleterious outcomes and should be suppressed or outlawed, such as those craved by pedophiles, narcissists, sadists, fascists, and the like; although, they too are not to be blamed or praised for accidentally inheriting their particular cause-effect chain that caused them to be what they are and enjoy what differently-scripted humans consider perverted satisfactions.

"On the other hand, if you are selected by The Truther and you refuse to answer the three reality questions you will be fined the first time it happens; and if it happens again after being selected by The Truther, you will be banished from the group. This law is necessary to cause all members of this group process to make contributions.

"The bottom line is that it's OK to be wrong by saying something; but it's not OK to say nothing, if The Truther selects you. This is a form of lying by omission, a major sin in this process. Everyone knows something about everything, however irrelevant it might be in general.

"After experiencing the process for a session or two, persons violating process laws will be fined or required to leave the room for one hour at the instant of infraction, and if this does not result in causing the individual not to violate group laws s/he will be permanently banished.

"It takes a while for some people to get used to these laws, having never had an opportunity to function as an equal response-able member of a truly democratic process, most group processes having been contaminated by stroke-hungry greedy power-hoggers who control most of the airtime and strokes for themselves, forcing most members to remain silent while adapting to and obeying them and their irrelevant time-wasting rituals and pastimes; but after experiencing fully democratic processes most people can overcome their prior undemocratic programming and will appreciate being caused to lead when selected by The Truther; and they will find it satisfying when they succeed in inserting themselves in the process after the person owning the floor stops, thereby earning strokes, with no holding up of hands to get psychological permission and protection, thereby learning not to play psychological Games, i.e., not being forced to act out Persecutor, Rescuer, and Victim roles.

"It's against the law in this group to hold up your hand to force someone to rescue you or to force others to give you the floor because it's a deleterious use of power, not only reinforcing your weaknesses but debilitating the group by causing the group to lose relevance, effectiveness and efficiency. In this group you are all empowered adults, and you must assert your opinions whenever you are selected by The Truther, not to selfishly garner strokes for yourself or to Rescue others but to honestly tell the truth of the matter as best you can. This process has no gatekeepers tasked to Rescue, Persecute, or Victimize others, and no one can make a fool of anyone.

"In this group all equal members are paid to work in uptime to succeed during the sessions, not to withdraw into downtime or to create noise by holding up hands and gossiping.

"There are other laws of the process, such as no libeling, slandering, or cursing. Negative allegations about any person, including public figures such as politicians, celebrities, and prominent citizens, should be backed by fact and evidence, at least approximations about the when and why of the lies, anti-social behavior, or criminal actions allegedly occurring, and something about the mainstream or internet media in which it was reported. Unfounded malicious libelous defamatory allegations and conspiracy theories spread by word of mouth in scurrilous ways are not encouraged in this process. Talking in this group with the intent to foster bigotry, hatred, and irrational discrimination is outlawed."

Dr. Logger's long-winded dictatorial monologue about democracy bored, rattled, confused, and upset several people in the group, making them wonder whether they could put up with his arrogant demeanor for one meeting, much less any number of them. No one in the group had ever experienced a group like this before.

Most of the members sat looking at the floor in front of them, with several thinking Logger was a hypocrite, preaching democracy while telling them what to do and think like a fascist dictator, talking down to them.

Several minutes went by.

Logger matched and paced the body signals of the group members, saying nothing, attempting to out-passive the group, to force someone to respond to the issues Bubba had led the group to think about and discuss.

Maria, exasperated, finally blurted out, "This is unbelievable. You come in here and start laying down rules and laws like we are a bunch of criminals or school children. You have not furnished us any written documentation for anything, no agenda, no syllabus, no handouts, no background reading of any sort, and then you start talking to us like we have no rights. No one can learn like this."

Rout—"I'm sorry you feel that way Maria. You are free to leave at any time if you seriously disagree, but the laws of the course are what they are. They are necessary to guarantee our discussions will be full, free, fair, frank, democratic, and effective. They insure respect, dignity, and equality for all group members. You are being well paid for your time and work. As of now each group member has received a five-thousand-dollar payment for today's work. You may resign from the process at any time and you may retain whatever payments you have received up to that point as the process unfolds. The laws of the process, however, are not subject to democratic argument, and they will not change. Plato had this same problem back in ancient Greece. Read his *The Laws* for background. This group will not operate like the US Congress.

One of the paradoxes of democracy is that you have to have dictatorial fair rules and laws laid down by lawgivers in order for democracy to function efficiently and effectively. There are of course many forms of democracy, but here we will use the form of democracy deemed most efficient and effective by me and the process donors, who are paying you for your time and participation. It's our way or the highway."

This comment escalated the dismay of the group.

Several more minutes elapsed with no one saying anything. Most members sat stone-faced glaring straight ahead not making eye contact with anyone.

Finally, someone said something.

Harrison—"Now see here, Rout, this is no way to run a meeting. You've got to take charge and follow an agenda. You've got to call on the most qualified people to talk about things. You can't just point out people to say things by a damn spinner rooster or let just anybody say whatever he wants to, which by the way is a damn insult to my intelligence. What do you think we are, a bunch of kids playing Spin the Bottle? You've got to assign the problem to your best staff people so they can make a power point presentation to fill everybody in. This is ridiculous! Especially sitting in a circle like this. You need to have your people set up in chairs in neat rows and columns. You're supposed to be the leader, out front, taking charge. You can't avoid your leadership responsibility by spinning an arrow to make people talk, not calling on people, not even allowing people to hold up their hands, while you sit around twiddling your thumbs just like everybody else. You're trying to make people say something whether they want to or not, no matter how unprepared or unqualified they might be."

Rout—"You have got a lot to learn here, Harrison. For starters, you are not the boss here. In a pure democracy anyone can speak up and say what they think, and has a responsibility to do so. I'll grant you using The Truther to select people to start discussions does not occur in most democratic processes but the founders of this particular democracy decided after weighing the advantages and disadvantages it is best to randomly select leaders to start discussions, to insure every member has an equal chance to be the leader of the discussion, otherwise certain members will cow others into submission and control the agenda so as to achieve their selfish ends at the expense of others. As to setting the room up in orderly rows and columns military style, such a layout might work best in dictatorial Parent-Child fascist groups and organizations such as large business corporations like yours; but that kind of classroom layout cannot come close to competing in terms of efficiency and effectiveness with the circle discussion layout in Game-free democratic I'm OK—You're OK Adult ego state groups and organizations.

"Randomly selecting people in a democracy is not a new idea. Greeks used it to select leaders as early as the Sixth Century BCE. The process is called sortition.

"People who rise through the ranks in large fascist corporations do so by adapting and flexing to and doing the bidding of authoritarian bosses to survive. Otherwise, they get fired. There is no democracy with rights of membership under a rule of law. They are psychologically enslaved to a boss. Large corporations are fascist dictatorships. The main thing that counts in a corporation is pretending to agree with and pleasing your boss, doing her or his bidding, living up to his or her expectations, commonly called ass-kissing and brown-nosing, not thinking for yourself, obeying the reality principle, aka doing what you gotta do to maximize your chances for the short and long run in the case you find yourself.

"The bad news is that succeeding in many organizations, maybe most, does not require learning the overall truth about anything. What it requires is learning what your boss says the truth is, and being willing and able to do it acting as if you believe it. This is true in most organizations, whether they be small businesses, corporations, school and university systems, religions, militaries, political parties, street gangs, etc.

"This group for sure is not like a large authoritarian organization such as a corporation, a fascist dictatorship antithetical to democracy, where dependent humans are enslaved to a boss, who has the right to fire subordinates for any reason, and nobody has a right to freely speak her or his mind about anything, even if they hold up their hands. I know many of you in this group are opposed to the idea of democratic Game-free discussion processes using Adult—Adult transactions, but if you stick with this program long enough you may learn to respect true democracy.

"I am talking about transactional analysis psychological Games here. A Game-free discussion process is one in which there are no Persecutors, Rescuers, and Victims. We'll be hearing more about this as we progress in our meetings. Adult—Adult transactions happen when members of the group have their Adult ego states cathected, or activated, as opposed to their Parent and Child ego states. The Truther cathects, or turns on, Adult ego states. Most transactions in large corporations are Parent—Child transactions at every level of the chain of command, the boss cathects a Parent ego state to dictate something and subordinates are forced to cathect Adapted Child ego states to respond. We will learn more about this as we go along."

Harrison—"You mean you think you can teach *me* to respect your idea of democracy."

Rout—"Yes, if you stick with the program longenough."

Harrison—"Well, I'll assure you, that's a mighty big if. I run a business and for sure I do not need your five thousand a month. I can walk out of here at any time. I make over twenty times that much per month already. I came to this meeting out of curiosity more than anything else, and I think I have about learned enough. This is a lunatic fantasy of some sort. And furthermore, my friend, you are badly out of line. I will not tolerate your insulting attitude."

Rout—"I'm sorry you feel that way about it, Harrison. Thank you for your candor. There's the door, if you want to leave now. There's one thing I agree with corporate bosses like you about, it's my way or the highway regarding democratic process rules and laws that must be obeyed. We have employed private security professionals to escort anyone out the door if he or she threatens me or anyone in this group."

It got so quiet in the room you could hear a pin drop, and another ten minutes elapsed with nobody saying anything. Rout decided to move on. He told the group most discussions normally lasted about one hour after The Truther was spun, since after about one hour discussing a problem most groups generally got bored with the point or problem under discussion and wanted to move on. He said they had barely scratched the surface of a good discussion of the issue Bubba raised, namely whether the economy was the biggest problem in the world, and if so, what to do about it. He told them since they were beginners he would ask Bubba to spin The Truther to select a new leader so they could move on. He repeated the rule for spinning The Truther: The last person selected will spin The Truther next.

Bubba demonstrated his disgust and contempt by slowly swaggering toward The Truther rooster in the center of the room. He twirled it in a dramatic fashion causing several group members to flail and jerk around with spontaneous body movements, causing some to make scurrilous sarcastic contemptuous comments to group members around them.

Rout then reached down and pulled a cowbell from his briefcase on the floor, which he vigorously shook, creating a loud clanging sound that quickly jerked the group members to attention.

Rout—"Several of you are violating the no gossiping law. Do not do this again, or punishments provided under the law will be administered."

Hal—"I thought you said the no gossiping law only applied when someone else was talking."

Rout—"No, it applies during the entire three hours of a session, including time members spend spinning The Truther."

The Truther selected Trudy as the new leader. She wanted to know if she was supposed to comment about what Bubba had said or bring up a new topic. Rout said he didn't care, that she should do whatever she thought most appropriate, since she was now the Leader of the Moment. She then said she agreed the economy was a serious problem but it was so general that she did not have much to say about it. She said she thought civil rights were equally important, that women were entitled to equal pay for equal work and should be free to choose abortions. This produced about thirty minutes of discussion with several citizens saying what they thought. When the discussion ran out of steam Trudy twirled the arrow and selected a new leader. The next leader, Margaret, mechanically defined a problem, listed two alternatives, and perfunctorily gave a recommendation. This produced a new silent spell. Rout thought more should be said about the issue Margaret brought up so he refrained from ordering a new Truther twirl. About two hours of the first morning session had by then elapsed.

Nobody said anything for about forty-five minutes, up to about noon, so Rout told them they were on their own until two o'clock. He told them to enjoy their lunch and report back promptly at two o'clock for the afternoon three-hour session. He told them coming into any session late without a valid excuse was also against the law, and violators would be prosecuted. Rout told them violating this law, or any of the process laws, could result in a fine that would reduce their monthly compensation and could cause their permanent banishment from the group.

Rout said there was one additional law he probably should alert them to at this juncture. Stonewalling is illegal. He said if it appeared to him that members were deliberately not saying things to psychologically collude with other members to passive-aggressively undermine and sabotage the process they would be fined or banished. He said he realized some people just naturally talked more than others and some members would naturally speak up more than others, but passive-aggressive stonewalling, lying by omission, deliberately not saying things attempting to cause others not to say anything to undermine the effectiveness of the process, was illegal. He said lying was also illegal—both lying by commission, by telling deliberate falsehoods, and lying by omission, deliberately withholding relevant thoughts, ideas, and information to play Games.

Most members by then were shocked, disoriented, upset, or infuriated, but no one said anything as they left the hotel. Outside they scattered like a covey of flushed quail.

Bubba and Henry were walking down a sidewalk heading in the same direction.

Bubba—"Can you believe that shit?"

Henry—"Hell no! This takes the cake. Who does that asshole think he is?"

B—"Hey, why don't we find us a bar somewhere and have a beer."

H—"Good idea."

B—"By the way, my name's Bubba. What's yours?"

H—"Henry."

B—"Glad to meet you, Henry."

After taking his first swig of Pabst Blue Ribbon beer, Bubba popped a question.

B—"How much longer you gonna stick with this crap?"

H—"I don't know. I thought it was crazy from the git-go. We still don't know who's payin' for this or what they're up to. This has got to be a scam of some sort."

B—"Or a bunch of liberals, nuts, communists or something. One thing's for sure, though, they've got more money than sense."

H—"Yeah, the money's real. At least so far. That's what got me. I couldn't believe it when $50 popped out of that ATM machine. Did they deposit $100 in a bank account for you like they did me to sucker you into this thing?"

B—"Yeah, that's what got me too. And then after I told them I would come to one meeting they put a fucking five thousand dollars in the account. I don't know what they woulda done if I hadn't showed up, which I thought about. But then I got to thinkin' if them damn fools put five thousand G's in my account once they might do it again, for one day's work, or whatever you want to call what this crap is."

H—"That's pretty much my story. Reckon how long they'll keep it up?"

B—"Don't know, but, as obnoxious as that Logger shitass is, I'll probably stick with it a while longer, so long as they keep a'handin' out the money."

H—"Me too more than likely. I've got too many bills piled up to turn it down. Wonder what that rich sombitch who said he makes twenty times more a month than they are paying him is gonna do? Reckon he'll drop out?"

B—"I bet he don't. But he shore got pissed."

Over sandwiches and another beer,

Bubba—"I don't know what's worse, having to sit for three hours without a break, or puttin' up with that smartass attitude, or that damn spinner. Calls it a truther, for god's sake, a fuckin' rooster crowing its head off. Can you believe that shit? Spinnin' that damn thing to make people talk? Hell, it's a damn insult. That is a nice-lookin' copper rooster though. Sounds like my rooster back home."

Henry—"You got that right, but the asshole just sittin' there sayin' nothin' is even worse. Can you imagine him just sittin' there for damn near an hour with nobody sayin' nothin'? With the rest of us setten' there not knowing whether to shit or go blind—and there's some smart people in there, one guy's a doctor—and nobody sayin' nothin'. God amighty."

B—"I know. It's like he's payin' us to waste our time to put up with him, or maybe he just wants to make fools out of us or somethin'. It's damn weird, I'll tell you that."

H—"I wonder what he'll come up with next—bring out a bullwhip or chains or something. He's already got a cowbell. I tell you what, Bubba. I think I'm gonna go back to my room and call my wife and maybe take a nap. We've got almost an hour before we have to show back up."

B—"Good idea. Enjoyed talkin' to you."

H—"Yeah, me too."

Most of the members went their separate ways after they left the hotel, having no desire to talk with anyone, feeling drained, confused, and angry. Most found a deli, pub or restaurant a few blocks from the hotel and ate alone. On the other hand, two other small groups congregated. Most of them had about the same sentiments as Bubba and Henry regarding Dr. Rout Logger. No one had anything good to say about him, considering him arrogant, unfeeling, and dictatorial. Maria said he was dehumanizing. She said he said he believed in democracy but acted like a fascist, making up rules right off the top of his head whenever he felt like it, like an absolute dictator. A few members cut him a little slack, thinking he might know what he was doing.

Almost all the participants thought about dropping out, but concluded they would be paid well for six hours of misery, bullshitting, discussing, or whatever you wanted to call this. A few knew they could not attend all the meetings even if they wanted to because of previous commitments; but they were curious to learn what would come of this. Some thought they could turn Rout Logger around and teach him how to act like a decent human being.

About half the members wondered what to do with the two hours, which was more than enough time for lunch. Most of them staying in nearby hotels went back to their rooms to collect their thoughts and refresh themselves, some taking naps; others read, checked their email and made telephone calls. Some sat in the lobby of the hotel where the meeting was held and read. A few went shopping. Some took walks.

Several group members thought about asking Rout to cut the time for the lunch break to one hour so they could get off work an hour earlier. This would give them more time to catch earlier flights home after the meeting, as some had decided to do, not staying in a hotel Friday or Saturday night, having arranged early and late flights before and after the Saturday meeting, to save a little money and have more time with their families back home, while others wanted to stay in a hotel to give them time away from their families. A few brought their spouses along with them; two members brought spouses and children along for the trip, since they had never been to Louisville, Kentucky. Some had stayed in the Brown Hotel before and knew it was an old but good hotel.

Rout—"Good afternoon, folks. I hope you enjoyed your lunch. Some of you probably think I should have told you in advance what would happen in the meeting, and I should have passed out a detailed list of do's and don'ts, or a lengthy detailed printed set of instructions, perhaps passing out something like a syllabus for a college course, explaining in detail all the process procedures, rules, laws, requirements, and so forth in advance.

"The problem is I don't know everything that will happen as we progress through this process, yet I know I have to provide some structure. Any process requires a few procedures, rules, and laws to achieve a satisfactory level of efficiency and effectiveness. I'm sure I will invent a few more as time goes by, as they occur to me. Most likely if you stick with it you'll conclude the process is efficient and effective. Everything I said this morning was audio and video recorded and you can access it with your computer in this room before or after a session starts, if you forget something you want to remember. I have an assistant who can help you pull it up on your computer if you need help.

"Some people would call me a facilitator, but I am more than that. I do some teaching, but I am more a co-learner than anything else. Most of the problems we will be discussing do not have provably-true "right" answers. The best answers are those that have the highest probabilities of producing salutary outcomes. This process is analogous to some university business school case method courses, which entail analyzing and discussing facts, not memorizing theories, dogma, or doctrines, or talking about rumors, lies and conspiracy theories; but instead of discussing researched printed paper cases in a casebook, our case is what is going on now around Spaceship Earth itself.

"On the other hand, you may talk about your personal feelings and thoughts regarding the facts of Spaceship Earth in these sessions, as a client might in a group therapy session. We are interested in what you feel, think, know, believe, advocate, and recommend regarding factual problems threatening Spaceship Earth.

"You have now been furnished at your work station a seating chart showing the name and location of every member in the room, a UniDesk™, and a laptop computer.

"The computers will be booted up during all sessions from now on. You can adjust the UniDesk™ to position your computer to the height and angle that optimizes your comfort and efficiency using the computer as you sit in your chair. The desk was invented and trademarked by a former professor who used a similar process in his classes. The model used here was custom manufactured to fit our layout and chairs.

"A UniDesk™, an Apple laptop computer and a seating chart will be in place for your use in all subsequent sessions, as will one of the chairs in this room which will be moved from the hotel and city of the last meeting to the new hotel and city for the next meeting.

"We will use the computers to check out facts on the internet when we have disagreements or a lack of factual knowledge among group members regarding a particular problem or opportunity. When a legitimate question or dispute exists about facts the entire group will do an internet search for relevant facts. The default browser is Google because it is widely used and generally effective, and because I am used to it. Once someone decides she or he has found relevant facts he or she will email the website address to the group. Special email addresses have been arranged for every citizen in the group for use during group sessions. It is against the law to email anything to persons, groups, or organizations other than members of this group using these computers, and such emails have been blocked. You can only send content to the whole group in the meeting room at once. Again, there will be no side conversations during group sessions, including computer email conversations. "The Group" email addresses have been permanently affixed to the address bar on your email page. Just hit the "send" button one time to email the whole group. We use the same rule for email communication as for face-to-face communication: No gossiping of any sort is allowed during group sessions, by tongue or computer. Anything said must be said to the whole group. We will not use this Google/email process often, but we will use it when disputes arise about facts in discussions and when I decide you need information from various internet sites. I will tell you when to use your computer during sessions.

"I have also given some thought to using the computers occasionally to give you an opportunity to publish your own writing to the group. I'm not sure how this will work but it seems to me it might be helpful to set aside 30 or so minutes now and then for writing, posting and reading, to add variety to the discussion process. If there are any poets among you this will give you an opportunity to express your feelings and thoughts about what has been going on the group process in writing. All poems must relate to what has been discussed or experienced in the group process. This would entail stopping the discussion and giving each of you a few minutes, perhaps up to 30 minutes, time to compose something. Should you wish to post your writing to the group, you would save your writing in a Word document and email it to the group members as an attachment, which would be opened on all computers for reading and comments. This would give you an opportunity to express feelings and thoughts in writing in language not possible to express orally in the discussion.

"If you write something at home you want to publish to the whole group or forward something you have found on the internet at home you will have to transfer it to your group computer using a memory stick, and you will have to get my permission to do so. All you need to do is tell the whole group during a session what you want to transmit and I will decide if it's appropriate within the context of what we have been discussing.

"While we are on the subject of computers, why not open up your computer right now and turn it on? The power switch is a circle button to press at the upper left of your computer surface. There are only three icons at the lower edge of your screen, an internet browser icon, an email icon, and a word processing icon, which are all we need for this process. If you hit the browser icon a Google internet search slot, as well as other browser options, will appear at the upper right of your screen. When we do internet searches to find facts, all you need to do is type your questions regarding the problem in the Google slot and hit the return key to find the addresses of Internet sites with information relative to the problem. If you find a site with relevant facts, copy the Internet address and paste it into an email—all emails are preaddressed to all group members, and only group members, which are the only addresses you can use as recipients. After it appears to me you have had sufficient time to find relevant addresses, I will notify you to send the site addresses you consider relevant to the group, which all of you will do simultaneously, which will result in each of you receiving a list of sites sent by all group members. I will give you a few minutes to visit and peruse some of the sites and digest the information. We will then discuss the information using our normal discussion process with leaders selected by The Truther. This should result in a factual discussion of the problem.

"Regarding the poetry, during these sessions, should I decide to do this, I will give you a few minutes to write and save your poem to a Word document, after which time I will tell you to attach your poem to an email and send it to the group. Everyone in the group shall then receive a list of all poems written and sent by the members. We will then discuss one or a few poems using our normal discussion process by twirling The Truther to select the poems to be discussed. It's ok for you not to post any of your poems by the way. It's ok for none of you to post any, for that matter, should I decide to do this, the purpose of the exercise being to give you an opportunity to abstract in a philosophical artful way your experience in the group and get feedback. All poems posted must relate to experiences shared by the group. All posted poems will be saved and some of them might be posted in the Spaceship Earth Group book published around Earth based on the discussions and proceedings of the group at the termination of this program.

"During the morning session I heard some cellphones go off. This is also against the law. All cellphones must be turned off during all sessions. And for sure it is against the law to play on your computer for your own entertainment during a session, searching for irrelevant information on Google, such as information for your personal business. At no time are you to do anything with your computer unless I tell you to, and I must authorize all questions you are to find facts for with a Google search. You many suggest questions and fact searches to the group, but I must ok the computer search. We cannot waste the time of the group with frivolous irrelevant computer searches just for the fun of it.

"Don't get caught with your hands on your computer except during authorized times. If you do you can be fined or expelled.

"You may not remove a computer from the discussion room for any reason. Our support personnel will pack up all computers, UniDesks™, seating charts and chairs after the afternoon session each month and have them ready for your use at the city and hotel of the next monthly meeting. Do not write or doodle on the seating charts. The computers are not personalized, so do not save any sort of personal messages, notes, etc. on them. The relevant thing is the discussion, the entire content of which is being saved through the audio/visual recording system.

"On the other hand, the web addresses and facts of all internet sites used for internet facts found and accepted by this group as relevant in its discussions shall be saved.

"Make sure you are sitting between the two members the seating chart says you are sitting between in sessions for a good while, so all group members can learn your name to be linked to your face and what you say. After the group has had time to learn the names of all participants I will from time to time require everyone to move to a different position, maximizing the distance between you and the two people you are now sitting between, to eliminate any psychological collusion and alliances that may develop between group members.

"You are not to remove a seating chart from the room for any reason.

"Although it is not my job to teach you, I decided during lunch to share more background with you. I know most of you are wondering why you were selected and where the money is coming from. You were selected from a large pool using computers and the internet, based on information available through internet surveillance systems, much like the government uses. The sponsors know a good bit about you. You represent a cross-sample of the culture, from various socioeconomic and educational levels, representing various professions, occupations, vocations, religions, political parties, racial backgrounds, and sexual identities. About one-fourth of you are registered Republicans and about one-fourth are registered Democrats. The rest of you are Independents, Greens, Libertarians, Progressives, tea partiers, and some other things, including non-voters. All major religions are represented among you, as are non-theists. All of you are at least reasonably bright.

"As you know, this process could cost a considerable amount of money if it continues for a long time, especially if it expands into other countries. Monthly expenses for this group currently are about $260,000, over three million dollars a year. Where is the money coming from? It's coming from anonymous donors who pledged varying amounts, some large, some small. Why did they do it? These people are seriously worried about Spaceship Earth, a planet supplied with oxygen and various gases and elements necessary for sustaining plant and animal life by natural physical and ecological processes in a closed system hurtling through infinite time and space in concert with gazillions of other inter-galactic and inter-universal objects. The sponsors think serious changes must be made to stop and avert extinction processes and events caused by global warming and the possibility of nuclear war, caused by greed and lust for power, income inequalities, poverty, racial hatred, class hatred, religious hatred, nationalism, ethnic hatred, cultural hatred, overpopulation, resource depletions, and poorly regulated economic systems, whether capitalism, socialism, or communism.

"The donors think *homo sapiens* on Earth will not change their economic and political systems unless they learn new ways of feeling, thinking, believing, communicating, and behaving, and they do not think mainstream media, schools, colleges, universities, churches or governments can produce this kind of learning. They want to see if this process can cause you to learn what might save Spaceship Earth. They know you would not pay to receive this sort of education, so they want to see if you will assimilate and accommodate this sort of learning if they pay you to do it. The whole thing's an experiment.

"The donors do not think human Earthians will voluntarily learn new feelings, thoughts, beliefs, dogmas, doctrines, and behaviors on their own, especially if they have to pay for it. They want to know if human Earthians can be paid to learn what is necessary to save Spaceship Earth. You are their first class of guinea pigs. If it works, they intend to roll the program out to other countries, as extensively as possible, depending on how many more donors they can find to fund programs. If what you feel, think, say, do and learn in this program produces salutary results it could help save Spaceship Earth by creating this sort of learning process in groups around Earth.

"At present about sixty-five thousand Earthian species become extinct every year, and hundreds of thousands have already become extinct on Earth. Our job is to hopefully come up with something that will prevent the human species on Earth from joining all the other extinct Earthian species in a cosmic happy hunting ground. An Earthian is an individual member of any species of fauna or flora now alive on Earth.

"The appellation Spaceship Earth, by the way, was invented by Buckminster Fuller back in the 1960s. For background you might want to read his book *Operating Manual for Spaceship Earth*. Fuller also invented the word *Earthian*.

"There were some similar programs back in the 1960s and 70s that people paid to attend, but they mostly died out as the culture changed after 1980, after the Ronald Reagan presidency turned back the clock in the US, not quite as much as the Taliban turned back their clock in Afghanistan, but a serious cultural regression occurred nevertheless. Fewer and fewer US citizens will pay for bottom-up personal growth, encounter group, brainstorming or pop psychology programs anymore, largely caused by anti-intellectual top-down messages and requirements produced by the regressive culture. More and more poorly informed fearful citizens bought into conservative right-wing ideologies and fantasies, eschewing more than ever facts, logical reasoning, social and psychological innovations, and scientific discoveries.

"We are paying citizens to participate in our progressive discussion process, which is devoid of doctrines, dogmas and rituals, focusing instead on relevant factual problems and opportunities, hopefully generating workable consensual strategies that will help sustain Earthian life indefinitely.

"Any questions?"

Bill—"I gotta ask. Why did you choose these Apple Macintosh computers?"

Rout—"Because I have been using a Mac since they first came out in 1984, and I still think they are the easiest to use."

Bill—"I beg to disagree, and I teach computer science."

Rout—"You're entitled to your opinion."

Maria—"During lunch some of us decided it would be better if the lunch hour was only one hour long so we might get out earlier so we might catch a plane back home on Saturday, to attend mass, or church, or whatever on Sunday morning, to have more time with our families. Would this be permissible?"

Rout—"No."

Hal, the last person selected by the Truther, got up from his chair and did his duty, spinning The Truther one more time, after Rout caught his eye and diverted its gaze to the center of the room.

The Truther selected Adam.

Adam—"This is the most insane seminar I can imagine, but I guess I might as well try to say something relevant. The biggest problem is there are so many problems it is almost absurd to waste time talking about any one of them. Most people do not want to hear or talk about real problems. They're zombies numbed and dumbed down by irrelevant crap since childhood. Somehow most kids learn how to read, write and do simple arithmetic in grade school, but not much else. I was talking about this with my wife a few days ago, telling her I could not remember learning a damn thing in grade school in any class. I could remember playing with some blocks as if they were musical instruments in a music class and filling out some sort of work sheets in another, but that is about it. I can't remember a single discussion about anything in any class. Relevance was irrelevant. Most of the time the teacher just seemed to sit behind her desk and stare at us. I do remember one teacher teaching us how to eat soup using pencils as simulated spoons and her coming up behind me and showing me how to do it holding my arm and telling me to dip into the soup from the inside out and raise the spoon straight up to make sure it doesn't spill.

"But I swear that is about all I can remember learning in a grade school class. Somehow, I learned how to read, write, and do arithmetic during those years, but I cannot remember learning any of it in a class. I remember looking at a few books with colored pictures about Jack and Jane doing things in simple declarative sentences that were supposed to help us learn how to read. High school was not much better, but there were two courses in which I remember learning something, plane geometry and physics. And I did learn a few lines of one or two of Robert Burns' poems in a literature course, and a few lines of a poem called Invictus.

"If you take the average person today, even many college graduates, all they care about is watching movies and television, especially soap operas and sports, and playing video games. Rarely is there any serious discussion of economic and political problems. As I said they're zombies. And they vote, if they vote, that is, for zombie politicians who tell people platitudes, fantasies, and dogma they want people to hear. God forbid a politician would talk about or seriously analyze facts about real problems.

"So the biggest problem is ignorant and stupid voters. I recently saw George Carlin on tv telling his audience, 'Stupid people vote for stupid politicians; it's as simple as that!'

"How you would ever educate enough voters to cause them to vote for intelligent, wise politicians who would vote to raise the taxes of large corporations and the elite rich, create infrastructure jobs to create jobs for the middle class, and scale down the US military-industrial complex?

"But that's what needs to be done, among many other things, such as doing things to reduce the threats of global warming and nuclear war. It's depressing as hell. What are the chances any of this will happen any time soon? Probably about zero. So here we sit waiting for some catastrophe to happen, as most people just blithely tend to the details of their daily lives as if there were no threats at all, some looking as if they are happy. Ignorance is bliss I guess."

Dick—"Come on now. You know that's not right. I'm a politician and I know I talk about relevant matters with my constituents. Here you are lucky enough to live in this great land of ours and all you can do is complain. America is the greatest place on Earth, blessed by God with the greatest values on the face of the earth. If we stick to our beliefs and values the Lord will guide and protect us. If we continue to love Him, in His tender mercy, he will see us through and welcome us into his heavenly home. Have you accepted Jesus into your heart? If not, as a true American I say unto you it is time you got right with God, before it's too late."

Adam—"I can't believe right off the bat in this lunatic seminar I get confronted by a moral moron politician. All I did was speak the truth as I see it and I immediately get chastised by a religious nut who believes a god will take care of everything. If he does why is it he let this mess we are in now happen? Must be a very incompetent god. You people do not have enough sense to get in out of the rain and I know it does no good to argue with you. You don't want to be confused by facts or logic. All that count are your so-called values which most of you preach but do not practice. If a god is going to take care of everything, when is he going to start? Why did he allow things to get as fucked up as they are in the first place if he takes care of things? I have never seen one shred of evidence with my two eyes that any sort of god has ever done anything on Earth, regardless of what people believe or do, or say, or pray."

Dick—"I can see you need some praying for my friend; but don't you ever call me a moral moron again. I won't put up with it. You have insulted me and my religion, which is against the laws of this group. What about it Rout? Tell this liberal creep he can't insult me or anyone else in this group because of their religious beliefs."

Rout—"Well, you may be right. Religious nut may be a bit strong, Adam. On the other hand, Adam was making the point that people who ignore facts because of their ideologies are morons, which sounds ok with me. On another hand, you just called him a liberal creep, which most people would consider insulting."

Dick—"Anyone who criticizes my religion, my beliefs and my values insults me. I won't put up with it I tell you."

Rout—"You don't have to if that is what you believe. Anyone can drop out of this group at any time. There's the door. But if you're making a threat, that will not be tolerated. Don't forget, we have security people available if we need them to enforce rules and protect the group from violence."

Dick was angry and confused, shocked by Rout's response. He decided Adam must be a damned atheist. He considered getting up and walking out but he remembered the five-thousand-dollar monthly fee, which he needed. He wondered how many people in the group were like this asshole. Adam's reactions were like Dick's in some respects. Did he want to put up with this? Yes, at least for now, because the money was too good to turn down. Adam was pleasantly surprised by Rout's reaction to Dick's comments; but he wondered where were the security people? Were they somehow observing and listening to the group? Most of the group members had similar feelings, reservations, and questions stimulated by Rout's comment about the security system, which made most of them feel less secure. They felt trapped by what looked like some easy money.

Looking out the window of the plane on the way home, Sam, like most of the group members, wondered what he had gotten himself in for. He thought the project sounded interesting and he was impressed in some ways by what he had seen and heard. He was impressed by the UniDesks™, the computers, and the seating charts, which made it easy to link names and faces, and the overall efficiency of the process. The leather arm chairs were comfortable. He liked the way Rout had laid down the law, although he agreed he had been a bit short and discourteous with a few of the group members. But he thought he had generally been fair and impartial. He thought using a Truther to randomly select leaders was a novel idea and was surprised by the dynamics it caused in the group. It did seem to cause them to talk in a more adult way. For sure The Truther engendered feelings of equality and fairness among members. It insured those with domineering or manipulative personalities would not completely take over.

He had never seen a group composed of people from backgrounds as different as those in the group. It was clear some of the people in the group were wealthy and others were poor; some were highly educated and some were not. There were several shades of skin color, ranging from almost black to almost white. It would be interesting to see what would happen in the group, making different people talk with one another like equals, but he had little confidence anything significant would happen. What could they produce or learn that most people did not already know? He still found it hard to believe donors would spend this kind of money on this sort of thing.

On the other hand, if only the country could operate like this, he thought, there would at least be a chance people could work out some of their problems face to face. One of the problems with the way things work now is that people are separated into their groups and cliques and churches based on their wealth, skills, and beliefs, doing the same things day after day, talking with the same people day after day. They might become more skilled and expert in what they do and they might become more confident they are right but they would not be doing anything to make sure the whole system survives. The better they became dealing with their jobs, lives, and communities, the worse it might become for Earth as whole.

Sam had been worried for some time about the possibilities of global warming. People were now talking more and more about human extinction, the human species becoming extinct within decades. Yet most people just keep on going as if nothing is wrong, feeling, thinking, and doing pretty much like they always had. Just a normal change in the weather they say. How this group could solve this problem is something else, but at least they might talk about it, and this might at least cause them to vote for politicians who might vote for things that might help stave off horrible consequences. Or is it already too late?

Sam was already in his late seventies, and he knew he would not be around much longer. He knew he would soon be personally extinct regardless of what happens to all Earthian species. And sometimes he wondered if he cared. He had by now learned enough about ageing to know it's not fun, prostate cancer, diabetes, high blood pressure, skin cancer, arthritis, allergies, glaucoma, worrying about falling and breaking a hip, getting ripped off by pharmaceutical and health insurance companies, hearing and reading about more and more old friends and relatives dying, no, not fun at all. But there were still a few satisfactions. He loved being with his wife, beautiful scenery, birds, trees, streams, sunset views. He enjoyed good food and a glass or three of red wine. He took satisfaction from making a little money in the stock market now and then, however dissatisfying it is to think about a real estate holding that may be unsellable, without almost giving it away, thanks to the Great Recession of 2008, and the probability of a similar crash at any time. He enjoyed talking with his son and his grandchildren and learning about their experiences and achievements. In many ways he knew he was one of the lucky ones.

He would probably do what he could to hang around Earth as long as he could, however much of a drain he became to his healthcare and retirement system, finally wasting away in a nursing home if he lived that long. But he thought one strong heart attack causing him to die in his sleep would be a good thing. He had made out his will as fairly as he could and he was ready to go when his lights went out.

Meeting with this group gave him something new and interesting to do in the meantime.

SESSION TWO
SAN DIEGO, CALIFORNIA
NOVEMBER 2019

Rout—"OK, ladies and gentlemen, let's get down tobusiness. Whoever The Truther hit last spins it next. By the way, there is one more rule. If The Truther stops between two of you and it's not clear which one is closest to the line of fire The Truther will be spun again."

No one recalled immediately who had been hit last, as they looked around at one another with quizzical expressions. Finally, someone said, "I think it was that lady over there."

Julia—"Yes, come to think of it, I think it was me," so she got up, walked to the center of the room, and gave The Truther a spin.

The Truther selected Stuart.

Stuart—"As I understand it we are supposed to bring up some sort of problem and then say what we think is the best alternative for solving the problem, is that right?"

Rout—"Yep, that's it."

Stuart—"Well, I'll tell you what's the biggest problem for most college students like me. It's college loans that most of us are taking out to go to school to major in something knowing there may not be a job after we graduate, especially a job in the field we majored in. Most of us are having to work part time to get by, if we can find a part-time job. You don't have time to study and you don't have free time. It gets to you after a while. As far as alternatives are concerned, one would be to drop out of school and go to work full time if you could find a full-time job, but what would that lead to? Everybody knows you can make more money in the long run if you have a college degree. What would I recommend? Tough it out and stay in college and hope for the best, I guess."

After about two minutes elapsed with no one saying anything, Rout told the group he hoped they did not repeat the silent spells of the previous session, that it was their job as individuals to dive in the discussion as soon as the selected leader finished his or her spiel. He said the time would pass faster if they cooperated. Again, he said, there could be no holding up of hands. Just dive in on a first come, first serve basis. He told them to "just come out with it," and remember you don't have to be "right". He said it's almost impossible for anyone to know "right" answers for general economic, political, social, and psychological problems. But he said they should try to be right, saying what they really thought was right, and that it was far better to be honestly wrong than to be dishonestly right, that is saying something to please someone for some sort of favor knowing full well what you said was right was bullshit.

Barbara—"Well, I'll say something about this, since I have a daughter in college and I know something firsthand about the predicament this young man is in. My husband and I have three children, two still in in high school. My husband earns a good salary but we still have trouble making ends meet. Every penny we take in is budgeted. We are not able to save anything and we often dip into what meager savings we have to make ends meet.

"We help our daughter all we can but she too must rely on student loans to stay in school. She's an English major. She says she wants to be a writer, but she could teach after she graduates. We wish her well of course, but we wish she had majored in something more practical. One thing we have learned is you can't tell your children what to major in in college. And here we are with two other children who want to go to college. I agree with this young man, Stuart, the best thing is to do whatever you can to finish your degree, and deal with the debt as best you can. That is you, isn't it, Stuart? That seems to be you according to the seating chart."

Stuart—"Yes, for sure that's me, all right, and who are you? I can't tell by looking at the chart."

B—"I'm Barbara. I sit between Albert and Ron, according to the chart."

S—"Oh, yeah, I see you now on the chart. Thanks for your comment."

Rout—"The more names you get to know the easier it gets to know where people are coming from. All of you surely know by now my name and the names of the people on each side of you in the circle. All you do to identify someone is count the number of chairs between that person and me on the chart, assuming you are all sitting where you are supposed to be sitting, between the same two people you were sitting between when we established the seating chart in the first session. Count the number of people between you and me on the chart and make sure you are in the right seat for the afternoon session, if you are not right with the process now.

"Since the seating chart was randomly established by going around the room giving one's name at the start of the first session, this-counting-spaces process is necessary to make sure you are sitting where you should be so everyone can get to know your name. As we progress from session to session your group imagoes will become clearer and more accurate as members are differentiated, that is you will learn to see them more as they really are instead of the way you assume they are now. A group imago is a mental image one carries around in his or her head of what a group is like and how it should be run based on experience, which most of the time is distorted when one joins a new group. The more you interact with a new group the more you see the group members for what they really are, not only knowing their names but knowing something about their ego states, scripts, transactional patterns, time structuring patterns, pastimes, Games, and so on.

"All of you made it back for the November session here in San Diego. We have had no drop-outs. I'm certain some of you will have to miss a session sooner or later for one reason or another. If that happens make sure you leave a vacant chair where the absent person would have sat. That way everyone can still calibrate who everyone is by looking at the chart and would know who is absent. If someone permanently drops out or is banished, we'll make and issue new charts showing there is one less chair in the room.

"If you are not familiar with transactional analysis terms such as ego states, scripts, Games, and the like you might want to read *Born to Learn: A Transactional Analysis of Human Learning* to learn something about them as they apply to learning situations such as this one. You can find a copy of this book by typing the title into Google at any time. I recommend you use some of your five thousand per month fee to buy some relevant books. On the other hand, I have posted a list of references as suggested reading on your computer containing material about transactional analysis terms. Most of these terms are colloquial self-explanatory terms but it might help you to read up on them. Not required of course. Don't worry about having to pass any tests to participate in this group."

Sam—"Before we spin The Truther again I would like to make a comment about the problem of student loans and the problems college graduates are having finding jobs.

"I'm a writer and a social activist and Iread several internet and print journals dealing with economics and politics, including education problems, and I read recently there are more problems in higher education than student loans and jobs for graduates. During the last ten or so years colleges and universities have been forced to cut costs and increase tuition to survive. Students pay more for tuition and professors are paid less to teach. A much higher percentage of college teachers are now adjunct faculty paid starvation wages with little or job security. Many are so afraid of losing their jobs they have lowered their standards to produce higher grades for students who are learning less. At the same time colleges have increased the number of fields of study attempting to prepare students for jobs, some of which are very narrow or vocational, and worth little in the job market. About the only ones coming out ahead in the last ten or so years have been the administrators and coaches. There are now more of them relative to professors and they are paid more. While fewer high school students can now afford to attend college, a higher percentage of students are resorting to student loans with relatively high interest rates, which are profitable for lenders. Some economists are now saying we have an educational bubble, which could burst like the housing bubble of 2008, if more and more students do not repay their loans, in which case student loan rates could increase even more. College enrollments, like housing construction after 2007, could plummet, causing untold problems for college and university budgets. It's not a pretty picture. Assuming this is true, it may be colleges and universities are in about the same position as college and university students, having little alternative but to keep on doing what they have been and hope for a better day. Like many organizations these days they are caught in a Catch-22 situation.

"What would I recommend? Just keep doing what you are doing as long as you can, I guess. Seems like more and more people are being put in this position. More and more businesses, governments, and everything else for that matter. All "Earthians" I suppose."

Rupert—"No doubt about it, the hope for a better day strategy is the number one strategy. As a banker, I can tell you that's what most people are using right now. They come in to our bank and want to borrow money to keep on doing what they have been doing when they can't pay back the loans they have now. Very few have viable options for doing anything else. A lot of people accuse us bankers of not lending money to people who need it and hoarding money the government gave us after the 2007 meltdown. Well, it may look that way, but that's not the way it is. We would be more than happy to loan out all the money we have at decent interest—if we thought borrowers could pay it back.

"The housing bubble came about because bankers loaned money to people who could not pay it back, when the loans were sellable to other suckers up the chain. Bankers could take a profit on the bad loans and get them off their books, by packaging them and selling them to others. You can't do that anymore. Bleeding heart liberals in Congress put pressure on Bush I, Clinton, and Bush II to create rules so unqualified borrowers, called subprime borrowers, disadvantaged people, could buy houses so they authorized Freddie Mae and Freddie Mac to buy up securitized bad loans, leaving banks with some profit for bonuses for their executives and leaving the loss with the government and US taxpayers after 2007.

"Up to 2010 banks could do the same with guaranteed student loans, billions of dollars of which are still unpaid on the books, with decent interest, around 6 percent. The government quit this program in 2010; now they make direct loans to students, still at relatively good interest of around 6 percent. About 70 percent of college students have student loans when they graduate. The average loan is about $30,000, which is not too bad if the student can get a decent job after graduating, about like paying off a car loan. On the other hand, I heard about some young man who borrowed about $100,000 staying in school long enough to get a doctor's degree and he couldn't find a job once he got the degree. That would be like paying off a starter house you could not live in. Nobody knows how many of these millions of student loans will ever be paid back."

Stuart—"Well, I can tell you I intend to pay mine back. I guess I was one of the lucky ones. My parents have helped me some. I have been able to find some part-time jobs and I only owe the government about ten thousand dollars. I'll graduate in a year with a degree in electrical engineering, so I ought to be able to get a job; and if I get to keep on coming to this monthly meeting paying me five thousand dollars per meeting just for showing up, I'll pay off my student loan and have some savings in the bank before I graduate."

Horatio—"You don't have to have a college degree to get ahead, if you're willing to work hard and take a chance. I started out in 1990 flat broke with no college education and no debt working construction. I learned carpentry, plumbing and electrical on the job and became a contractor, building houses and apartments, owning apartments, and renting them out. I had to borrow a lot of money from banks but I had a good credit rating and I always paid it back. I worked 14-hour days seven days a week, almost never taking a vacation. I now own a couple of convenience stores, a couple of restaurant franchises, and rental property all over town. I don't think all this government help is necessary for college kids or anybody else. If the government would just get off our backs and let us alone we would all be better off."

Ellen—"With all due respect, sir, I think you're wrong. I graduated from college over a year ago with an accounting degree, supposedly one of the best degrees there is for getting a job, with over a 3.5 g.p.a., and I still have not found a job. I have interviewed over 20 firms, with no offers. I am beginning to think I am overqualified. Seems all they want are people who know how to save people money by lowering their taxes.

"And about half my friends graduating when I did do not have jobs, and most of the others do not have good jobs in their fields, many just part-time jobs to get by. The problem is there are not enough jobs out there. I heard recently in Washington, DC they opened a new Wal-Mart with 600 job openings and over 60,000 people applied for them. That's one out of one hundred who got accepted at a Wal-Mart, applying for low wage jobs that will not make you a living. That ought to tell you something. No matter how hard and long you are willing to work if there are no jobs you are out of luck."

Horatio—"I sympathize, my dear, but you are young and beautiful and you have your whole life before you, enough time to get whatever you want. All you have to do is be patient, and good things will happen for you."

Ellen—"That's easy for you to say. You probably have no idea what it's like to go around from interview to interview and get rejected time after time, by people who don't seem to like their jobs but who are afraid of losing them, knowing there are millions of people in the US out there looking for work, nine million I believe it is. It's depressing not being able to find a job, but it's also depressing knowing you probably would not like the jobs you are getting turned down for."

Horatio—"You're probably right about that. When I started out with no college I did not interview that many people. I took the first job I was offered, in construction, about the only job I ever interviewed for, and I stuck with it till I went out on my own. But I still say you will find a job sooner or later with your education and accounting skills, and all unemployed people if they are willing to apply themselves and build what they now call skill sets can also find jobs."

Luke—"Do you pray? Have you asked the Lord to help you in your hour of need. Jesus said, "Seek and ye shall find; knock and it shall be opened unto you.""

Ellen—"To tell you the truth, no, I have not done that. If I thought it would do any good, I would do it, but I have never seen anything like that happen for anyone I have known. If Jesus cared about unemployed people, and if he had the power to do something about it, why hasn't he already done something about it? Or is it he wants to force the unemployed to beg him for his help in some sort of prayer?"

Luke—"The Lord works in mysterious ways. I will pray for you."

Ellen—"Gee, thanks."

Things got quiet again. About seventy percent of the members agreed with Ellen; about fifteen percent agreed with Luke.

Rout—"Several of you have been engaging in unlawful covert communicating, smirking, grimacing, chuckling, sighing, jerking your heads and necks around, and what have you, letting possible co-underminers and agitators around you know of your surprise, dismay, disapproval or approval. This process is not like the US Congress or a high school class. Agitators and underminers will not be tolerated. Cliques will not be allowed to spontaneously form in this group. If you are not interested in or disagree with the speakers and the proceedings in this process that is your business, but you must keep it to yourself unless you socially communicate such decisions, reactions, feelings, opinions, etc. to the whole group.

"It's ok to daydream to tune out speakers and the proceedings provided you look straight ahead or down at an angle so as not to create distractions around the room, thereby luring your neighbors into joining agitating undermining psychological cliques.

"It's ok to say whatever you want in this group, provided it is not obscene, threatening, or slanderous, so long as it is socially said to the whole group at once; but you cannot say anything unless you say it to the whole group.

"Those engaging in unlawful covert psychological communicating today were recorded on tape. Your fines for today's infractions will be deducted from your next monthly bank deposit.

"Ok, let's break for lunch."

Just when it seemed the group might have settled in for a spell of OKness Rout once again destroyed any peace of mind the group might have achieved by telling them certain ones would be fined for covert communicating. The members again left the room in disgust and dismay wondering what to do about Rout and whether to put up with his rules and procedures. Several members decided to have lunch with one another. At least they could clique together outside the group and covert communicate all they wanted to.

Maria—"I was beginning to think Dr. Logger might have some human decency in his soul after all, but then he says he will fine us for merely looking at one another and sighing. Why I have never heard of such a thing. It's atrocious. Something has got to be done about this."

Nancy—"But what can we do? He is probably a total jerk. I can't believe he's got a doctor's degree. I just don't think a professional that cared about people would carry on like he does. How old would you say he is?"

Ellie—"Probably about 50 I would say. Old enough to know better than to say and do what he does. I'm a teacher and I can tell you the man is abusive. He's not caring. He has no regard whatsoever for our feelings. If I were to do what he does in my classroom I would have parents complaining to my principal in a heartbeat. And I can tell you parents would be out to get him. The very idea, telling grown men and women they can't even laugh or smile when they feel like it. I'm probably one of the people he was talking about fining for smirking. You bet I smirked, and I had a right to smirk at some of the idiotic comments that were made in there today. And the attitudes! Can you believe how that old man talked to that poor girl?"

Helen—"I agree Dr. Logger is off the charts for arrogance, but, being a nurse, I can tell you most doctors are arrogant. They all start out idealistic after getting out of medical school, driving a Toyota to work, and that sort of thing, and treating nurses with respect. But the older they get the more arrogant they get, talking down to people and driving Cadillac's to work. I've seen it happen over and over, and there's nothing you can do about it, except quit your job."

Maria—"I work with doctors myself as a social worker, but I don't think most of them are like Logger. Besides that, he's not a real doctor. He does not have an MD degree. He has a PhD in management science, whatever that is. Most real doctors show some respect for their patients and are decent human beings. This jerk seems sociopathic, devoid of empathy for others. And this system of his violates basic human rights. He's abusive, that's what he is, and his whole system is abusive. He thinks he can force you to do things, even force you to talk, fining you for things. But the worst part is the system he uses to spy on us and control us. Can you imagine taping and filming everything people do in that group? Why it's about as bad as the US government spying on people collecting emails, telephone calls, and what have you using the surveillance systems of the FBI, CIA, and the NSA. In his room you have no freedom whatsoever. You can't even use body language to express your feelings. I think this should be against the law, the real law, the law of the land, not the law of this maniac."

Nancy—"I would quit right now if I could afford to. But I can't. I don't make that much money as a hairdresser, and I have a young daughter to look after."

Maria—"You're a single mother?"

Nancy—"Yes. And it's not easy to make ends meet, especially when the work slacks off. I've had to rely on food stamps at times."

Helen—"I can understand that. My husband has been out of work for over a year now, and we have three children."

Ellie—"A lot of people are going through hard times now."

Maria—"I know that, but we still can't let this monster get away with his atrocious behavior. We've got to do something."

Ellie—"I hate to say it, but I don't think there is much we can do about it except grin and bear it for a while, or quit. Maybe he'll lighten up or something. If you go to the police and report him, if he is breaking the law, the money will dry up. They have already paid me ten thousand dollars in two months. I don't want to give this up."

Nancy—"Me neither."

Maria—"I for one don't intend to put up with this."

Helen—"Well, good luck. But sometimes you have to let it go, give it up, whatever, and just get along as best you can."

Back in the meeting room.

Rout—"Have any of you written any poems about the process so far you would like to share? If you have type them into your computer now and email them to the group."

A few members said they had composed a poem about the group process but could not remember it now. Rout told them they should remember their poems when they happened in their minds. Several members had trouble finding the power button on their computer and some had problems opening the email program to type in their poem in the email message block. Rout told them how to do it and told the group it was ok to show members needing help on your right or left in the circle what to hit on the computer if you knew how to hit something and your neighbor needed your help. Rout said they could use their word processor to compose the poem and send it email as an attachment if they wished.

Everyone understood how to write something in the email message block and send it to the group after the initial discombobulation with the computers subsided. Many of them began to type something into their emails. Most were happy they were being allowed to play with their computer for a while, having been given some respite from the threat of having to talk, if The Truther landed on them.

After allowing them about thirty minutes to write something, Rout said, "OK, that's about enough. Now email your poem to the whole group. All you have to do is hit the send button. The email program already has everybody addressed. There's no need to worry about typing anything in the subject line.

"All right, it appears everyone who wants to has now sent in a poem. So now open the email message in your inbox. You will see the poems everyone just sent. Read the poems and select the best one in your opinion. In a few minutes I'll tell you to vote for the best one. Once all the votes are in we will recognize the poem receiving the most votes.

After about thirty minutes elapsed,

Rout—"OK, let's vote. Just type the name of the best poem in your opinion on your email window and send it in."

In a few minutes,

Rout—"The poem receiving the most votes was composed by Clarence. Here it is."

"Unbelievable"

We knew not
What we got
In for
Signing up,
For what this is,
A fiendish trap
Filled with crap,
To warp our minds,
With all kinds
Of tricks and taunts,
Lured from familiar haunts,
Paying us with dope,
With little hope,
Wages five grand a shot,
Which is not so hot.

Rout—"Any questions or comments."

Hal—"I've got one. Your poem-evaluation process is nonsensical. There is no way anyone had time to read all those so-called poems and make a fair selection."

Rout— "Ain't that a shame. OK, whoever got hit last spin The Truther and let's move on."

The Truther rooster landed on Napoleon.

Napoleon—"I can tell you nobody ever accused me of being a poet or knowing anything about poetry, but Clarence's poem seems OK to me, a good report on our situation. What are we supposed to do here, anyway, Doctor Logger? Do you want us to go through your three steps, or what?

Rout—"Include the three steps in your response if you wish."

Napoleon—"The problem is this outfit lacks a clear mission, there's no chain of command, no assignment of duties, no esprit de corps, and no leadership. It short it's a disaster. There's only one alternative. I recommend disbanding the outfit and sending the troops home. How's that?"

Another silence ensued. The members sat there looking straight ahead, apparently waiting for Rout to say something. After 20 minutes elapsed Maria erupted, leaning forward in her chair, looking directly at Rout.

Maria—"I think you are trying to drive us all crazy. You are responsible for this group but you don't act responsibly. You abdicate your responsibility as the group leader. You just leave us hanging. No structure. No guidelines. No information. No support. Look, I'm a social worker. I have an MSW, a masters of social work, and I know a thing or two about groups and group dynamics. I have had courses and workshops in it and I know the first thing a leader is supposed to do is provide psychological protection and safety for all group members. You are not protecting anyone. If anything, you are exposing everyone by stripping them of their psychological defenses. What sort of training do you have in group dynamics?"

Rout—"I have had courses and workshops in organizational behavior, group dynamics, psychotherapy, gestalt therapy, neurolinguistic programming and transactional analysis, with over 35 years' experience teaching and applying techniques from these fields in formal university courses in classrooms and by conducting workshops and consulting programs in small businesses and in large corporations. Here is a copy of my vita I just emailed to all of you. I assure you I am not trying to drive you crazy. Quite to the contrary, I am trying to drive you sane. While we're at it, how about the whole group looking at my vita. You will see it in your email inbox."

Maria—"But what has any of this got to do with the poem? I thought we were discussing the poem. You know as well as I do the poem was talking about you, so I am talking about the poem. Everybody here thinks you are a lunatic or fiend. The poem used the word fiendish, clearly related to you and your behavior in this group."

Rout—"Of course it does, but so what? Anyone who has had experience working with organizations and groups knows the formal leader of the group, if he is to be effective, must be capable of enforcing basic rules for the group, and, ideally, the leader will have had experience and training exceeding that of the members, and, if a group is to produce results, that is, productive changes, the leader must know and introduce things considered new and different by the members, which always causes some insecurity and fear in members initially, before they learn how to assimilate and accommodate the new learning. If this process is effective members in this group will learn something they do not already know, thereby developing better imagoes and personality adaptations as well as more comprehension of states of affairs, thereby becoming more confident, functional, and productive than they were initially. In the meantime, as anyone who knows anything about organizational life knows, the formal designated leader rules the roost, and it's my way or the highway regarding fundamental rules and laws. Once again, I repeat, if you are unwilling or unable to adapt and flex to my group imago and personality, there's the door.

"A group imago by the way is the image someone carries around in her or his head about the way a group or organization should be run. Both you and Napoleon have group imago conflicts dealing with my group imago because of your prior experience. Since I am the designated leader of this group it's your job to adapt and flex to me, not the other way around. Like it or not, students cannot teach the teacher how to teach. This is not a military outfit or a social welfare system. No one in this group is on welfare and none of you need the protection and commands of a social worker or a drill sergeant.

"Are there any more questions or comments about the poem? If not, let's get back to work. But first I want everyone in the group to look at my vita that lists my education, training, and experience. It should convince you I am well-qualified to run this group."

Adam—"Before we do, Rout, could I make a comment or two about your vita?

Rout—"Ok."

Adam—"On the whole your vita is an impressive list of accomplishments and it does show you have had relevant education, training, and experience in fields relevant to what we are attempting to do here. But it seems to me it is not as impressive as most people might think. Seems to me you are basically an academic and I suppose it's normal for us academics to list what we have published, including articles and books we have written in our fields, which is fine, but are most of them serious achievements? Most of us pretty much preach to our own choirs. Here you are preaching to people from a lot of different kinds of choirs. I noticed you have published in the *Transactional Analysis Journal*, which is the refereed professional journal for the TA field, but most of your articles, published in other fields, such as economics and management, have not been in Class A journals. Also, many of your articles were published in Proceedings papers of conferences, which have high acceptance rates, many of which are little more than the equivalent of term papers written by undergraduates, mostly busy work, not read by anyone but the author, the editor, and conference discussants. While you are successful in your field you are probably not as successful as most people in this room might think you are based on this vita, some twenty pages long, not being academics and not having seen academic vitas before. Most resumes used in the real world for job applicants do not include jobs completed. They just list the education, job titles, dates of employment, and so forth of the applicant, usually one or two pages long. Your vita is about twenty pages long, implying you have accomplished a great deal relative to people in non-academic fields, which is not necessarily true. If a building contractor were to list every building he ever built he too would have a long resume."

Rout—"You're right on, Adam, good point. Maybe it would be a good idea for you to share your academic vita in economics to give the group some perspective on this issue. You can download it from a memory stick at our next meeting and share it with the group. On the other hand, I think my general assertion here is valid: My education, training, and experience should have qualified and equipped me to manage this group more than most people."

After about five minutes of silence,

Rout—"OK, let's move out. Napoleon, spin The Truther."

Hal became the new Leader of the Moment.

Hal—"I must say, this Truther does keep your energy level up and your adrenalin flowing. You have no idea what is gonna happen next.

"As to problems, as I think we mentioned in passing in the first session in Louisville, the problem is there are so many darn problems in the world today it's hard to single one out as the problem you should talk about or try to do something about first. As Bubba pointed out when he got hit it's hard to know what is the most relevant problem in the whole damn world. I think most people most of the time visiting with friends or whatever ignore the world's problems. I think if you bring up a serious economic or political problem at a dinner party, or over lunch, in mixed company, most people will think you have broken a serious rule of etiquette, or , so most people have little experience talking about serious problems with groups. As an attorney I talk with clients about serious problems all the time, damn relevant to their lives, such as not getting screwed in a divorce or a land deal or something, but it's not talking about serious problems affecting the whole world.

"So a relevant problem for most of us in this group is that we have had very little experience talking about the world's problems in a serious way with anyone. Hopefully Rout here can teach us something about how to do this. But I think he said one of the reasons they decided to set this group up in the first place is that such groups do not naturally happen in the real world.

"Ok, that's an aside. Here goes at talking about the most relevant problem in the whole damn world, right now, taking a wild-assed guess….

"And the problem is—drumroll please— evolution itself. I happen not to believe in free will. I think all effects have causes, even effects such as human feelings, thoughts, beliefs, decisions, wants, and actions. You think you are causing yourself to think and feel and decide as you are now in reaction to what I am saying using free will? Wrong. I am causing you to feel, think and decide as you are by what I am saying. And what has transpired in this group process has caused me to say what I am saying now. That's not free will.

"True enough, what you are now feeling, thinking, and deciding depends on previous facts, theories, beliefs and decisions that came to be recorded in your brain, but I caused you to think about it by what I just said.

"And what I have said was caused by what you have said in this group, and by Rout's rules and procedures, especially his Truther, which required and gave me permission to say something, anything, that resulted in what I said.

"This not only happened to me, it happens to everyone everywhere. What you feel, think, say, and do depends on causes in your environment, what you are exposed to, and previous recordings in the brain. "It not only happens to you but to every man jack, woman and child alive on the planet. Therefore no one is responsible for what is now going on around the world. Everybody is just like you and me in the way they are caused.

"You think you just spontaneously-like feel, think, etc. whatever you feel, think, etc. whenever something happens? That you just poof as if by magic cause your reactions to happen out of thin air when something happens in your zone of consciousness?

"How can a non-caused cause happen? Think about it. Nothing causing you to feel or think in your brain what you feel or think?

"I don't think it can happen."

"Just a minute here Hal!", Luke bellowed.

"You are talking heresy. There is nothing in your brain but you and your Lord, who watches over you at all times, who knows your every feeling, thought, and act even before you do.

Nothing is causing you to do anything but you. You have free will. The Scriptures are very clear about that. Almost nothing is more sacred than free will, which our most merciful Lord God bequeathed to us. As much as Adam and Eve disappointed Him there in the Garden, he never gave up on us, and he is ever hoping that all His children shall repent and worship Him in His heavenly home."

Rout—"Let it be known Luke is out of order and shall be fined for interrupting the previous speaker. Let Hal, the previous speaker proceed until such time as he decides to stop of his own free will, or until such time as something inside his own head causes him to stop talking."

Hal—"Well, I guess I was a little long-winded getting to my major point, which is, since I think everything has been caused by evolution, everything that happens is inevitable, or depending on your perspective, accidental, and all species on earth are victims of circumstance. But I also believe if all people try to figure out answers for problems and tell others what those answers are this could cause things to get better on Earth. The problem is there are so few humans doing this sort of thing there is little chance humans alive now can change major causes of things, and the human species is doomed. I'm talking about poverty and income inequality, global warming, and that sort of thing, since most humans will just proceed on the evolutionary trajectory fate caused for them through infinite cause-effect chains.

"Therefore, the most relevant problem right now on Earth is there is nothing causing right answers to happen for problems such as the population bomb, global warming, environmental pollution, and climate change. Humans are checkmated as it were.

"I must say, I admire Rout and his people for setting up this group and causing us to at least think about and discuss relevant problems threatening all species on Earth.

"Thank you for giving me the opportunity to speak my piece."

Luke—"You, sir, have had your say. Now it's my turn. If there is no free will there is no right and wrong, no sin, no righteousness, no virtue, no real reason to live, nothing to live for of any significance. Can you imagine what the world would be like if there was no free will? Why men would live like savages or beasts, satisfying their baser urges and lusts at every whim, murdering without a pang of conscience, since guilt would not exist.

"How especially can you as a lawyer not believe in free will? The entire legal system is based on free will, otherwise how could you ever convict anyone of anything, hold them responsible for their crimes, and send them to prison, to pay for their crimes?"

Hal—"I beg to differ Luke. You don't have to have free will to have a legal system. If anything, we have a legal system because free will does not exist. If we had free-will we would have almost no crime, since most people are intelligent enough to know they ought not to commit felonies and serious crimes, especially since they know you will go to jail if convicted of committing them.

"No, we have legal systems, purely and simply, to cause people not to commit crimes, which it does, within limits. Most people have been caused to know they will be punished if they violate laws, and are aware of most of the criminal laws that can get them sent to jail. Most of the unknown laws are business laws that result in fines and other punishments where ignorance of the law is no excuse, which is why you need to hire a lawyer.

"People who knowingly violate criminal laws do not decide using spontaneous free will to violate the law; a belief, a previous decision, an idea, something, already caused to be recorded in their brains causes them to react as they do at the time the crime is committed.

"At the time a crime is committed, an enticement, threat, insult, whatever in the environment may be the main cause of the act. Previous beliefs, ideas, knowledge of laws, and so forth caused to be recorded in the individual's brain may not be sufficiently strong to stop the individual from committing the crime.

"But a pure spontaneous act of free will did not cause the crime to be committed.

"Regardless, it's moot what the cause of someone committing a crime is; if convicted you get punished anyway, and this causes less crime to be committed than would otherwise be the case."

Luke—"If that were true then nobody should be sent to jail, since it's not their fault if they don't have free will. That would be unfair."

Hal—"You're right it's not their fault they did what they did, but unfortunately mankind has learned over millennia that lawbreakers have to be punished to prevent crime, crime being defined as breaking laws.

"Speaking of unfairness, how fair is it for your god to sentence one of his so-called children he supposedly loves so much to an eternity of torment in hell for breaking his laws or commandments or not living up to his expectations? Seems to me that's irrationally harsh, especially when in most cases the miscreant was never arrested or punished at the time of infraction, or even warned he or she had better not do it again when he did it?

"You are a retired minister, aren't you?"

Luke—"Yes, I am, but my god is a god of love, who sent his only Son Jesus Christ to save sinners, who called men to save other men from hell, which was a merciful act. Since God gave man free will and knowledge of right and wrong people should be rewarded or punished for their acts on earth by God after they die. I shall pray for you."

Hal—"Go right ahead but I personally have not seen one whit of evidence that praying ever caused one single event of any sort to happen on Earth that would not have happened anyway. Something causes preachers, priests, and ordinary people to pray for sake of praying, which produces certain kinds of feelings, which could in some way cause certain behavioral changes, resulting in something, less crime perhaps. But it has nothing to do with free will."

Ellie then jumped in the fray.

Ellie—"Whether we have free will or not, we teachers are not allowed to discuss religion like this in our classes. We have something known in this country as separation of church and state, and I think we ought to keep religion out of this group or process, or whatever you want to call it."

Hal—"I hate to say it, Ellie, but I am afraid this is a symptom of the most relevant problem in this country in my opinion. If you can't even talk about what you think is most relevant what chance do we have we shall develop a fair and sane society. If everyone is afraid to speak out about what they think is most relevant, what is threatening the future of the country, if they cannot even say what they think ought to be done instead of what is being done by politicians and the government, what chance do we have?

"There is no doubt religion, or religious beliefs, is one of the worst problems in the world today. It's causing us not to deal with real problems threatening our existence."

Ellie—"How can you say religion is the problem when the whole purpose of religion is to help people cope with the problems of the world? Religion is here to help people, not make matters worse."

Julia—"Religion never helped me none. I could care less about it. I never talk about it and nobody I know ever does neither. I do my job and collect my money and I try to be a good person. Religion as far as I am concerned does not exist. It always did seem like mumbo-jumbo to me. Never could read the bible. Never did understand any of it. I work hard and I built my business up to where I make a living, and that's about all I have time to think about. I ain't gonna waste my time thinking about no religion. I can tell you that."

Another silence ensued. After about fifteen minutes Rout caught Hal's eye and looked at The Truther.

Hal got up from his chair, walked to the center of the room, and twirled The Truther. The rooster Truther crowed and Bob got selected as the Leader of the Moment.

Bob—"Wow, it is hard to figure out what to say when that thing lands on you with that crowing noise. I agree the worst problem when you get hit is figuring out what to say about any problem, there are so many of them. How are you supposed to know which is the most relevant problem economically, socially, and politically?

"In some ways my job as a physician is easy compared to this. When I sit down with a patient in most cases it's easy to diagnose the problem. The patient in most cases knows something is wrong because he has pain or visible evidence of some sort somewhere in or on his or her body. There's real pain or symptoms locatable around the body. Here's there's nobody sitting in front of you to interview and observe and there's pain everywhere, caused by ignorance, poverty, evolution, genetics, institutions, whatever.

"No matter what you say you're apt to make a fool of yourself. On the other hand, nobody can prove you're wrong.

"In my profession if you're wrong about what to do, especially if you do something wrong and the patient dies or becomes impaired or disfigured, it's obvious you made a mistake and you might get sued, in which case you had better be able to convince a jury you were not negligent.

"Here you can run your mouth all you want with little fear of punishment, as if running your mouth is doing something. I suppose it is, since it requires you to think some, and figure out what to say if The Truther picks you out. But any pain you might experience such as feeling bad about saying dumb things or making a fool of yourself, is not like the kind of pain I deal with in a doctor's office.

"So, to tell you the truth, I do not know what to say. I was always taught growing up there are two things you should not talk about in public: religion and politics. And I took this to heart. I almost never talked about such things, and still don't, especially with patients. Like Julia here I pretty much stuck to the straight and narrow growing up, doing whatever it took to learn math and science and make straight A's in college and get through medical school. And it never got much better after medical school. About all most doctor's do is work, spending almost all their time in their offices and hospitals, maybe taking off now and then to go fishing.

"So for sure, I am no expert on religion. I have no idea whether it would be better for us to talk about religion in here or not. I'm sure there are arguments both ways.

"I do agree with Hal, though, that religion is now a problem worldwide. All you need do is watch the evening news now and then to see the horrible effects religion is now having in the Middle East. You have got religious fanatics running around killing themselves and others because of religious beliefs.

"Thank a god we have never had anything like that in this country. On the other hand, look back in history, the Crusades, the Spanish Inquisition, the Holocaust, and what have you. No doubt about it, religion has caused a lot of violence and hatred.

"Religion is causing some of our political problems in this country, causing voters to be polarized, Evangelicals vs.

Episcopalians or whatever, causing politicians to be polarized in Washington, making it difficult to pass budget bills, making it difficult to pass a jobs bill, and so on.

"But would I recommend we spend a lot of time in here discussing religion, or trying to figure out how to change it, or try to create new ways of worshipping or dealing with religion? I don't think so. The probability of us coming up with anything that would change anything in this regard is low indeed, even if you used the internet.

"Religion has probably been one of the most discussed and argued about subjects in human history, and no one has ever proved anything. The probability of any of us saying anything in this group about religion that has not already been said is near zero. It's also impossible to prove anything about religion is wrong, such as whether hell or heaven exist, since no one has ever come back with proof. You can't prove or disprove anything about religion.

"So, I guess I would say that even though religion is one of the most relevant problems in the world today, we might as well go on to something else, since there is nothing we can do about it one way or another.

"Therefore, I recommend we move on to another subject."

Luke—"The Lord works in mysterious ways and He never said religion was provable. You have got to believe and accept His word on faith, and the word of our Holy Savior passed down to us in Holy Scripture. On the day of judgement the wheat shall be separated from the chaff, and the faithful shall receive their reward. Amen and glory hallelujah."

Steve—"The problem is we are losing our values in this country. We all know our values are the most important thing."

Martin—"I teach religious studies in a college and I can tell you you cannot teach values and religious beliefs to students in a state school as if you know the way the truth and the light. All you can do is teach the histories of various religions as best you can, based on the few facts that are known, such as when the religions probably started, something about the supposed founders, and so on. I am a strong believer in the separation of church and state, such as we have here in the United States, at least for now, which may not be for long, since some evangelicals and others are agitating to get rid of it. Americans have argued about religion from the beginning and some tried to force religion on Americans through the constitution, which did not happen. There has been much religious strife and controversy, but largely thanks to our constitution we have never had religious wars or persecutions, such as they have in the Middle East, or religious wars and violence such as what has occurred in France, Spain, and Ireland, Catholics vs Protestants, and whatnot.

"Most of our founders were deists, meaning they did not believe an anthropomorphic god exists, especially a vengeful, jealous or rewarding god, a human-like god, who looked like a human being, who could create a man and woman in his image in seven days. Deists believe their god is some sort of intelligence permeating the whole universe who set things up with physical laws and processes and did no more, letting evolution take its natural course.

"I think we should leave it at that and let everyone in this group and everywhere else believe whatever they want, and move on to something else, as Bob recommended."

Joe—"I ain't much on goin' to church. My folks never went to church and such and I don't neither. Couldn't afford fancy clothes for Sunday church goin'. I never sent my kids to church. But I believe in Jesus and the Fourth of July and them things that made this country great. I fought in Vietnam and I would do it all over again to protect my country. I taught my kids that and they believe it. They work hard like I do and they got pride in themselves and what they believe. Can't nobody take that away from us. God bless America and the American flag."

Julia—"I'm with you Joe. My folks was so poor we couldn't afford to go to church. Didn't have decent clothes and such to wear. Rich folks in church would look down on us. But we had an old Bible in the house and sometimes we said the blessin' before we ate. Folks like us needed a savior and Jesus filled the bill. Made you feel good to think that somebody really cared about you, and you was a'goin' to heaven after you died."

Martin—"Yes, of course, that has been the major appeal of Christianity, and most religions, throughout human history, and I would not want to take that solace away from anyone.

"But as you pointed out, Julia, and as Joe alluded to, Christianity in the US has often made the poor feel worse socially and psychologically because of not being acceptable in the first churches of the town or city. In some areas church services provided about the only venue in which the well to do could wear their new suits and ties and frilly dresses.

"I suppose we'll have to defer to Dr. Logger about how much we should talk about religion in his "process." What do you think about this, Dr. Logger?"

Rout—"This is not my process. I am paid to be here and coordinate the process, but I do not own it. On the other hand, I am just as entitled to speak my opinion in here as you are. I think religion has always been a problem and is still part and parcel of major problems around the world. On the other hand, I do not think religion is the major cause of wars. I think the main cause is most people not having enough and some people having too much. Religion evolved just like everything else. Homo sapiens have been on Earth about one million years. Organized religions only started evolving about five thousand years ago, the religions of Egypt and Assyria being the first, then Hinduism, Judaism, Christianity and Islam, plus many others at different times, and god knows how many sects, denominations, etc. of each one dreamed up at various times.

"Ever hear of the religion of Bill? I read about this in a Smithsonian magazine and it really happened. An American pilot during World War II crash-landed on a remote isolated island in the Pacific. The isolated natives there thought he was a god since he crash-landed in an airplane. Bill taught them a few helpful things on the island before he finally got rescued and taken back to his country. After he left, a male native declared himself the high priest of the Bill religion, indoctrinating children with Bill's beliefs and teachings. He included a major teaching that Bill would come back some day to save them. The priest built a church and conducted regular services and the worshippers of Bill participated in various rituals. Bill did indeed come back one day on vacation and his worshippers fell at his feet in awe.

"I suspect most religions got started somewhat this way, except nobody crash-landed in an airplane. The bigger, richer, and more powerful the country and rulers the greater the number of priests and preachers and the bigger and more elaborate the temples, cathedrals, and mosques. Some religions entailed erecting pyramids and large stone statues and monuments, as in Egypt, Druid Ireland, Mexico, and the Galapagos Islands.

"Unfortunately, we could spend several months or years discussing religion without creating or discovering useful recommendations or new rituals, so I suppose we should move on."

After slowly marching to the center of the room with his head bowed, Bob reverently twirled The Truther, and the rooster crowed, selecting the new Leader of the Moment.

Dan—"I'm an insurance man and a good Methodist, not an expert on religion by any stretch, but I would like to say something about it. For several years now I have been reading stuff on Facebook, and in the last year or so I have seen a couple of posts that made me think. The first one had to do with the writing of the New Testament. In this post someone said the Christian bible was written by professional writers commissioned by a Roman emperor, Constantine, in the fourth century after Christ was crucified by the Romans. According to this story the emperor was worried about the Roman Empire falling apart and he thought if someone wrote the right kind of book on religion he could use it to help hold his empire together, you know, make the population meek and humble, feel guilty for their sins, make them more obedient to him, that sort of thing. The bible quotes Jesus Christ saying people should render unto Caesar what is Caesar's and unto a god what is his, which would have made believers pay their Roman taxes and that sort of thing.

"According to this story the writers of the bible took stories that had been handed down for centuries about several religions that had saviors born of virgins that rose from the dead, and so forth, and wrote the bible, making it seem the bible and chapters in it had been written by people who knew and worked with Jesus. Now I have no idea whether any of this was true, but it always did seem strange to me there was nothing written about Jesus by his so-called disciples during their lifetimes preserved on any sort of writing material, such as clay tablets, parchment or whatever. Also, the stories in the bible about Jesus do not agree on certain supposed facts, such as whether Jesus was born in a manger.

"The second thing about religion on Facebook that astounded me is that a few years back this strange monument got erected at Elberton, Georgia with religious carvings on it and instructions for a new religion. The monument was made from huge granite slabs positioned together with a top slab, kind of like those giant stones at Stonehenge. In this new religion they recommended reducing the human population to five hundred million people and keeping it at that level forever. Regardless of whoever these people were, they believed five hundred million people was all Earth could sustain living in harmony with all other species.

"Now, how you could ever get the human population back to five hundred million would be a major problem, without dropping an atomic bomb or something. What is the human population now? About 7 billion, isn't it?

"At any rate, I recommend that a new religion be commissioned like the Roman emperor did along the lines of the carvings on this strange monument in Elberton, Georgia, with a required belief that women can only have one child each. That would cause the human population to peacefully shrink back to five hundred million people in a century or so."

Tony—"I hear crap like that all the time tending bar. People talk about religion a lot after they've had a few drinks. I've heard both these stories. I doubt either one is true, just more made-up bullshit."

Dan—"I know for a fact the story about the monument is true. You can drive out in the country near Elberton and see it for yourself. As to the story about the Roman emperor I'm pretty sure you can find sources about it on the internet. How about it, Rout, could we look this up on the internet?"

Rout—"OK, why not. It's about time we tried out our Google search system. Everyone, see if you can find proof this Roman emperor actually paid writers to write the Christian bible."

The group members then began to fiddle with their computers, turning them on, trying to find Google, preparing to make the search.

After giving them a few minutes to read some sources Rout wanted to move on—"That's about enough time for that. Dan, how about giving the Truther a twirl?"

It landed on Ron—"I drive trucks. Religion was always above me. Never understood it, for sure never studied it. Always believed in Jesus though.

"What do you want me to say about this? I asked Google if a Roman emperor hired people to write the bible and got about 15 million sources of information. Reading through some of them I saw several mentions of this Roman guy. I don't suppose that proves he did it, does it?

"I have no idea what to recommend about this."

Luke—"Thank you Ron, for your simple faith, and your testimonial. May God bless you.

"I also saw millions of possible sources about this subject, proving how important it is. I don't think any of them will change the truth of the matter, that Jesus is lord, and will save you from the fires of hell, if you will but let him. Amen."

Maria—"This is nonsense. You can't prove anything with the internet. Half of it is made up or lies. Fake news. Religion is a matter of faith, pure and simple, and you can only know the truth in your own heart."

Rout—"I also saw millions of possible sources, but it seems Constantine had something to do with the writing of one version of the bible in the 4th Century after the death of Christ.

"We could spend hours talking about nothing but this. How many of you think based on our first internet search that it is true Constantine influenced the writing of the Christian bible in the 4th Century AD? Let's see a show of hands?"

Most members held up their hands.

Rout—"OK, let's move on."

The Truther rooster selected Henry.

Henry—"Before we change the subject, I would like to say there are plenty of folks these days who do not believe in any kind of god or religion, at least not a normal kind of religion. Apparently, some scientists believe it is possible the universe just happened from, poof, a big bang, caused by nothing, a spontaneous explosion, ten to twelve billion years ago, spewing gases, matter, electrons and what have you in all directions causing billions of galaxies of stars to form, and gazillions of planets, including ours, Earth. I cannot imagine how such a thing could have happened but we know for a fact the universe exists and contains billions of stars and probably millions of planets. It seems obvious to me a human-like creature called god could not have possibly created the universe. If a god did it, he, she or it had to be nothing like a human being. There is no way in hell a human-like creature could do such a thing."

Rout—"Ok, any other comments about religion before we move on?"

Matilda—"There are people who believe there is a god but it is nothing like the typical god of a mainstream religion, a jealous, vengeful father-like figure making his children obey and love him to earn the privilege of living forever with him in heaven forever.

"They believe this god is rational and loves people unconditionally. They believe this god really understands why people do what they do, how they are caused to be what they are and do what they do, feeling sorry for humans, but not judging them, making no pretense of being all-powerful or all-loving, that sort of thing.

"Some of these people also believe in an afterlife of total bliss and happiness. Frankly, I don't believe in this sort of thing. I think when you die the electricity in your brain is shut off and nothing works from then on. You are like an unplugged computer, except your biological parts disintegrate and decay to nothing. It's like having a dreamless sleep from then on."

Luke—"I now see, my Lord, with all my heart, I am in the midst of unbelievers and deceivers, foolish men and women who dare to question your holy word thinking in their hearts they are superior to your word and your sacred gospels, full of pride and vainglory, on the road to hell. I pray for their immortal souls and I beseech you to have mercy upon them. In Jesus's name. Amen."

Steve—"For whatever it's worth, I don't think it does any good to talk about religion. Seems like no one ever really changes his mind about religion. People believe whatever their parents believed, they get brainwashed into it at an early age and they pretend to believe it from then on, however simple minded it might have been. I don't think most people professing to be religious really know diddly-squat about religions, or anything else for that matter. All they know are a few sayings they have picked up here and there, such as Jesus loves you and such, or hell is hot and you better get right with a god.

Almost none of them ever read the Bible they hold so sacred to see what it really says.

"I would like to bring the discussion down to earth and talk about what I consider the most relevant problem facing us today, the erosion and decay of family-owned small businesses in the US. I work in our family business. We manufacture metal stock tanks, hog feeders and other products for farmers. We have been in business over 50 years. I have a degree in business and I would like to continue the family business and pass it on to my children.

"Up to the past few years we did not have that much foreign competition, for various reasons, transportation costs were too high, foreigners did not understand our technology and processes, whatever. But now we do have foreign competition, thanks to NAFTA, the North American Free Trade Agreement, and we may not be around much longer. We still make a profit, albeit a declining one, and our sales are going down. It's almost impossible for small American manufacturers to compete with products made in low-wage countries.

"Thousands of small manufacturing businesses like ours have been driven out of business in the US since 1980, and especially since NAFTA was passed in 1993. And now we are confronted with problems caused by Trump's trade war that caused the price of some of our raw materials to go up, while giving little relief from our foreign competition in our markets.

"It may get to where there are no small family-owned manufacturing businesses like ours left in the US. Thousands have been wiped out in the last 30 years. I'm worried sick about it, worried about my future and our family and worried about the future of our employees, who we really do care about.

"Seems like there are no answers. The problem has been getting worse and worse for years and it just keeps getting worse. As much as I hate to say it, I think we would be better off with tariffs to protect our manufacturers and workers. There are billions of poor people in the world willing to work for a pittance compared to what Americans have been paid, and if you allow free trade around the world American wages will inevitably gravitate down to the lowest level, if the companies they work for can stay in business.

"This is already going on. We still have some car manufacturing in the US, but wages for automobile workers are now about half what they used to be. I read the other day an Indian textile company with 12 plants in India is now setting up a textile mill in a small Georgia town in the US to make yarn using American workers, in a town that had an American-owned textile mill up until five or so years ago. At the ground breaking ceremony with the Georgia governor the Indian owner of the new plant, to be built from scratch on some industrial park, said his people had figured out with tax breaks, low land cost, and transportation advantages they could make a profit using American workers still living in the town that were laid off five years ago. No mention was made of what kind of wages are to be paid, but you can bloody well bet they won't be as high as they were in the American mill that shut down.

"America is being third-world-ized. Wages in US manufacturing are being driven down toward the average level of the whole world, apparently now on a par with India. Maybe manufacturing will return to the US, but if it does, America will begin to look more and more like India, with a rich corrupt political and economic elite at the top, a small percentage of doctors, lawyers, engineers and such and untold millions of poor people living in abject poverty and squalor.

"Things got better in the US from about 1950 to 1980, but it's been downhill ever since for everyone but the elite rich, and it remains to be seen how far we'll fall before we hit bottom.

"I recommend bringing back tariffs to protect US wages and manufacturing, and punishing companies with much higher taxes for abandoning their employees and facilities in the US sending US jobs overseas."

Helen—"As you know nurses don't make that much money, and we work hard for our money. My take home pay has stayed about the same for a long time. I get a raise every now and then and I don't complain. I enjoy helping people. But I also don't need higher taxes and tariffs to keep my job. I worked to get an education and built my skill set to where I was worth something to an employer. Anybody in America can still do that. All it takes is being willing to work hard and get yourself the training you need to make yourself worth something to an employer. I don't understand why people expect taxpayers to keep on spending more and more money on welfare to help people when they can help themselves. I think we should lower taxes, not make them worse. And I don't think we need a minimum wage. You ought to be paid what you're worth, not what the government says you're worth."

Steve—"I agree with you about the minimum wage but I don't think the problem is people not being able to work hard and get training. It does no good to get training for a job that does not exist."

Jimmy—"I agree with you, Steve, about the working hard part, but I strongly disagree about the minimum wage part. As you may recall from our initial introductions, I am a labor union organizer. I deal with these sorts of problems day in and day out, and I agree with much of what Steve said about the most relevant problem today being the outsourcing of American jobs. Whew, where do you start? This problem has been around in some form, but it got going in earnest after Ronald Reagan got elected in 1980. The root cause is greed and inhumanity to man on the part of rich capitalists, not caring about your fellow man, only caring about your own selfish hide. On the other hand, you have the satisfied bystanders like Helen who do not have a clue what it is like to work in an industrial or big business setting as a wage earner alongside thousands of other workers doing jobs requiring specialized skills that can only be learned on the job. Most people who have never worked in places like this have no idea what it feels like to be treated like a machine and watched over constantly by a supervisor who is paid for his blind obedience to a boss who is paid a salary to force those below him, or her, to work as hard and long as possible, for as little money as possible.

"Skill sets, my ass, you don't need a damn skill set to work in most businesses as a worker. All you need is the ability to remember a few mental and manual manipulations peculiar to your job at the lowest level, which anyone can to learn on the job. And this is true pretty much all the way up to the top, except in staff areas, such as accounting, marketing, engineering, law and such. All general supervisors and managers all the way to the top spend the majority of their time simply watching others, bull shooting with cronies, brownnosing with bosses, and enforcing rules and regulations passed down to them by their bosses. About the only skill set you need is the ability to do what you are told. As to so-called higher order thinking skills, forget that. Nobody thinks in a corporation, except maybe those at the very top at times, but even they spend most of the time bull shooting and brownnosing, which are, I suppose, skills, the most important skills there are in business for those making the most money.

"As to being paid what you are worth, who the hell knows how much someone is worth? Do you really think you're worth

$5,000 a month to sit here and bullshit six hours one day a month? Give me a break! You are paid what you are paid because some idiot has decided to pay you that much, and this has nothing to do with what you are worth. Do you really think a corporate CEO can be worth $20 million a year? You think you are well paid at $5,000 a day? Some CEOs are paid $100,000 a day for bullshitting and brownnosing.

"Worth what to whom? You are worth a lot to your children and pets if you have any, since they depend on you and need you, but how much are you worth? Especially to a large corporation that could care less what you're worth, a heartless, soulless institution existing for the sole purpose of enriching its stockholders and higher management as much as possible by paying everyone else working for the place as little as possible, with every manager and supervisor in the joint being rewarded for putting the screws to everyone below them in the chain of command, or what I call the chain of obedience. You think corporations are free and democratic? Think again. There's almost no freedom or democracy in a corporation. Prisons are freer than corporations, since inmates in prison can think for themselves. Inmates in corporations can only think for the corporation. The corporation owns your mind and brain when you are supposedly at work, even after work sometimes. You can only think about what the corporation wants you to think about.

"Corporations are freer than prisons only in the sense workers can go home at night, and do whatever they want after they get home, and they can quit any time they want to, assuming they can find another job, which is damn near impossible for about half the people in the US right now, the employed half. Most of those out of work would work if they could find a job paying a livable wage. Most people working for corporations are not free to quit any time they might want to. Sure, assuming free will exists, they can quit any time they want to, and ruin themselves financially, but most people know they are not free to do what they always want to do. They have children to feed, clothe, shelter, educate, and on and. on.

"And those unemployed people are not unemployed because they are lazy and don't have 'skill sets. No, they can't find jobs because jobs do not exist. Some jobs do require so-called skilled sets, such as nursing jobs, and there are some openings for those kinds of jobs now in the US, and in IT and such, but I'll assure you there aren't enough of them. No, dammit, we don't need jobs requiring skill sets, we need jobs anyone can learn on the job that provide a decent income, like we used to have, if we are to have a decent country, like we used to have in the US.

"And I'll assure you, you need people like me who will work to make sure ordinary workers are paid as much as possible by people who are out to pay them as little as possible, and your real worth be damned.

"That's just the way the system works, my friends. The capitalist system that is."

Harrison—"I'm angry and insulted. I happen to be a corporate CEO and I can tell you this fellow is straight out of lulu land. Sounds like a commie. Yes, corporate CEOs are paid a lot because they are worth a lot. Most of them are so valuable they could leave at any time and find similar paying jobs working for competitors. The market sets the price for anyone in the real world. You are paid what you are worth in the market, and the only way you can find out what you are worth is try to sell yourself in the market. Whatever you are able sell yourself for is what you are worth.

"As to a union sympathizer like you being able to raise the wages of workers, you might be able to raise them to some extent in a company that has excess profits, but in a normally competitive business with a standard profit margin there is no way you can go in there and significantly raise wages without ruining the company. Significantly higher wages will cause the company to significantly raise prices for what it produces which will cause it to go broke because it won't be able to sell what it produces.

"If a company is producing something in global markets its labor costs cannot be significantly higher than the labor costs of any competing company in any country or it will go out of business because nobody will buy what they produce. Too expensive. If wages are lower in other countries than

US living standards if you have free competition then goods in that industry cannot be produced in the US or the living standards of US workers must be reduced to the level of the foreign workers they are competing with. That is the truth of the matter, my friends.

Jimmy—"I'm so sorry you're angry Harrison. It's a real shame someone as high and mighty as you would be subjected to my opinions.

"By the way, I'm a union organizer not a union sympathizer. As to your monetary pay being what you can sell yourself for in the market, I agree completely. If there are plenty of jobs your pay will go up. If there are no jobs you receive nothing, but that is not what you are worth as a human being, and what you receive has nothing to do with skill sets or what you are worth. You are a mere commodity paid what the market determines. Corporate CEOs are not paid millions of dollars per year for skill sets. They are paid as much as they are as bribe and hush money to make sure they enforce rules, regulations, policies, and procedures that enrich their higher ups writing their paychecks, making sure the higher ups are paid what they want at the expense of underlings in the system. In other words, CEOs are paid as much as they are for having a greedy grasping dependable loyal system, with respect to those who write the checks, not skill sets.

"As to no CEO being worth $100,000 a day, I could not agree more, but I happen to know some of them are paid that much, counting all their pay, salary, stock options, profit sharing, what have you. I saw in *USA Today* several years ago an article in which they reported some CEO had been paid $33 million that year. I figured out that was about $100,000 a day. How many days a year do they work, 300 maybe? You do the math."

Helen—"I don't believe it. Nobody could be paid that much."

Steve—"Well, I can tell you nobody in our family Subchapter S corporation makes anywhere near that much. I'll be lucky to take out $100,000 this year, as president and CEO, for a whole *year's* work.

"I agree part of the problem is that people at the top are paid too much, and that is a major part of the overall problem I brought up, but large corporation CEOs being paid too much is not causing family-owned manufacturing businesses to be wiped out."

Bob—"A lot of people think we physicians make a lot of money, but it's nothing compared to what some of these CEOs make. I saw on the internet the other day that the top six executives at Walmart had been paid some $116 million dollars in one year in what they called performance pay. That would work out to over $300,000 per day.

"The highest paid physician I ever knew was an old fraternity brother of mine, a cardiologist. He developed such a reputation as a chest surgeon that he could sit in his office and cut deals with rich prospective patients from all over the world. He said a billionaire once offered him so much money to travel to the home country of the billionaire to operate on him that it took his breath away. I assume it must have been several million dollars for one surgery.

"But I assure you that is not going to happen to most doctors. In fact some of them are having a hard time of it now, paying back their student loans and finding good situations."

Julia—"That can't be right. Why that's insane. Nobody could be paid that much for one day's work. You must have made some sort of arithmetic mistake."

Mikhail—"I happen to be an accountant, and I have my calculator with me, which I just used to do the math. If you divide $116 million by 300, which is probably about all the days a CEO works per year, the answer comes out to be $386,666 per day for six employees at the top."

Adam—"I think you have a pretty good grasp of things, Steve, especially your thesis that the worst hit of all have been small manufacturing operations in the US, that were essentially sold down the river by NAFTA and the World Trade Organization, and, I might add, by most economists and politicians.

"Adam Smith back in the eighteenth century published his seminal economics book *An Inquiry Into The Nature and Causes of the Wealth of Nations* in which he discussed the benefits of free trade among nations. He essentially argued all nations and peoples would become wealthier if free trade, and unfettered competition, existed among nations, since this would cause all nations to specialize in producing raw materials, goods and services at the lowest prices since competition would force them to produce what they had the greatest comparative advantage for producing, which would also cause the yearly output to be maximized, the assumption being the more goods and services produced, the greater the wealth of nations, and, presumably, the citizens therein.

"This makes for a good story and it made *The Wealth of Nations* one of the most famous books in history, the most famous economics book. It may be true that free trade and unfettered competition would maximize production, but we will never know for sure because it will never happen and never has happened. There have always been trade restrictions, tariffs, subsidies, quotas and what have you. Recent trade agreements have reduced or eliminated some of them, but free trade, even today is a myth. The US has all sorts of tariffs and so does every other country. NAFTA, the North America Free Trade Agreement eliminated some of them and bilateral trade agreements with China and others have eliminated some of them, and, it seems this has caused the problem Steve alerted us to, namely the loss of manufacturing jobs in the US, caused by smaller US manufacturing businesses forced into bankruptcy by foreign competition, and by the outsourcing of US manufacturing jobs by large corporations.

"Whether the elimination of trade restrictions has caused the wealth of nations to be reduced is doubtful. It may they have increased the wealth of nations and people. More goods may have been produced for more people.

"The problem for Steve and people like him in the US is that they paid the price of the progress. Their incomes and wealth went down so the incomes of and wealth of the poor in third world countries could go up, and so the incomes and wealth of American CEOs and stockholders could go up. The incomes and wealth of CEOs and stockholders of large corporations went up because of the outsourcing of US manufacturing jobs brought about by replacing high wage blue collar jobs in the US with slave-labor-equivalent blue-collar jobs in impoverished countries.

"Was this fair? Well, it turns out, fairness is in the eye of the beholder. Was it fair some of the dirt poor of poor countries should have their incomes increased by freer trade and competition between the US and its trading partners? Yes, of course. Was it fair the US CEOs and their bosses and stockholders who made this happen should have their incomes and wealth increased significantly, while workers of the US had theirs decreased? No, it's not fair, but that's the way things go under dog-eat-dog capitalism.

"Obviously, something went wrong, or maybe a lot of things went wrong. Should US tariffs be reinstated as Steve recommends to correct this unfairness? That is a tough one.

Maybe a little, maybe not, depending on how you look at it. But one thing is for sure; we need new rules and regulations to deal with this in the US, such as higher taxes on large corporations and the rich who reaped the windfall they fostered, and something should be done to improve the plight of those cast aside. We need a jobs program to provide decent jobs providing decent incomes in the US for those cast aside, ordinary workers, as Jimmy called them.

"I agree there is no way millions of unemployed people are going to learn new skills and magically find millions of unfilled job openings out there. This is absurd. Those openings do not exist. The jobs do not exist because aggregate demand is not high enough to cause entrepreneurs to create new products and services that would make enough jobs happen. The major problem since 1980 or so is that US economic policies enacted by US politicians have kept aggregate demand low, by decreasing the taxes of the rich and increasing military expenses, and not investing in domestic infrastructure and social programs, which has caused federal debt to explode. Monetary policy has been used instead of fiscal policy to take care of the real economy, the main street economy, not just too big to fail banks.

"The unemployment problem is actually much worse than the officially stated employment rate, since the number of people officially defined as unemployed by the US government is people currently looking for work, not counting those who know it would do no good to look for jobs that do not exist.

There are millions of unemployed people in the US who have given up looking for a job, who are not counted as unemployed. And there are millions more who would work if jobs existed. The actual labor force participation rate in the US for over ten years has been about 60 percent.

"The only way this can be cured anytime soon is by creating a massive government funded jobs program in the US creating infrastructure jobs that will put incomes in the hands of ordinary workers who will spend the money with small businesses, including small manufacturers and construction companies, that will create a multiplier effect sufficient to produce economic growth and full employment.

"Economic conditions during the Obama and Trump administrations markedly improved for the rich, and some jobs have been created for the poor, but the situation for millions remains dire. What's especially ominous is there are no signs the situation will be significantly improved for the middle and lower classes anytime soon.

"Unfortunately, most of the new money created by the Fed wound up in the hands of bankers and the rich, who saved the money, much of it being moved offshore to tax havens in the Cayman Islands and elsewhere. If you want to significantly stimulate economic growth and help the poor you need to put new money in the hands of the poor, not the rich.

"That's what I recommend."

SESSION THREE
ASHEVILLE, NORTH CAROLINA
DECEMBER 2019

Rout was beginning to have serious thoughts about the results of the program. It was obvious the group had improved its psychological and social functioning, agitations had diminished, and the group had become more cohesive. But so what? Was this a sign of significant change and progress or was it disingenuous adapting and flexing to make a buck? The five thousand dollars a month obviously was enough to entice them to attend the meetings but was participating in the meetings producing changes in their group imagoes, scripts, ego states, transactions, and general functioning? Would their experiences in The Group cause them to feel, think, and behave differently in other groups that would tend to cause polarizations to diminish in some way to help facilitate causations for the construction of consensual answers that would help solve problems posing existential threats to all species of fauna and flora living around Spaceship Earth?

Rout knew his supporters and donors would not continue to fund The Group indefinitely if there were no credible signs the process was producing significant changes in the feeling, thinking, deciding, and behavior patterns of the group members.

Rout had been concerned from the beginning about when and how to make a definitive judgment about how well the process was achieving its purposes, mission, and goals. While donors had been relatively easy to find to start the process, Rout knew there was no assurance the donors would continue to fund the process indefinitely. Although they had said very little up to this point, he knew they were bound to be getting curious. The donors had access to the transcripts and tapes and they could see there had already been changes in the feeling, thinking, and behavior of The Group.

For one thing, the donors could see that most of the group members now accepted Rout's leadership and they had accepted the rules of the process. Rout had proved the group process could cause group members from disparate backgrounds to at least pretend to change, at least when paid five thousand dollars for one weekend of time and six hours of group participation. It was a good deal for them, even apparently for the wealthy members. If the wealthy members did not need the money as they said, then the process was generating psychological satisfaction for them.

It was obvious most of the group members were by now gaining some satisfaction from participating in the process, especially being able to get away from their daily grinds to visit different cities. They were getting together in small groups for lunch and dinner, and while the groups initially formed based on verisimilitude with respect to various socio-economic criteria, the informal groups began to include individuals with different characteristics, apparently caused by feelings of liking and respect generated by the discussions, which was a good sign, indicating The Group would cause polarizations among people to diminish.

There were now fewer Critical Parent, Adapted Child, and Rebel Child ego states cathected and a higher percentage of the transactions were Adult— Adult and Free Child—Free Child. Every now and then they now actually had a little fun in the group.

At the same time the group had become more serious and business-like. The time of the discussions was now consumed with more work and intimacy with less withdrawal and fewer psychological Games. The content of the discussions had become more honest.

Rout now felt that he could make the case to the donors that the program was successful and had achieved what it set out to do. He was confident the donors had seen enough of the video tapes and transcripts of the group sessions to enable them to see for themselves what had gone on and happened.

The question now was where to go from here? Disband this group and start new ones? Pay the group members of this group to lead similar groups using Truthers in their communities? Expand to other countries?

On the other hand, Rout had read and heard about a mysterious new respiratory virus that had originated in China that was highly contagious and deadly. Would it spread to the

US? If so, would it be feasible for The Group to meet face to face indefinitely?

Rout decided to keep rolling along as they were for a few more sessions before making major changes in the group.

On the other hand, he decided today to give the group a reading assignment.

Rout—"Before we select a Truther-selected leader today, I have decided I would like to make a reading assignment.

"Please go to Google on the internet and go to the address I just emailed you http://www.effectivelearning.net/spaceship-earth--inc..html , and read "The Evolution of Spaceship Earth, Inc."

"I am going to set aside thirty minutes for everyone to read this article, at the end of which time we will discuss the article. We will as usual use The Truther to select the next leader of the moment to lead the discussion—What is the problem, what are the alternatives, and what do you recommend?"

3

WISHFUL THINKING

THE EVOLUTION OF SPACESHIP EARTH, INC.

I have argued at <u>https://blog.effectivelearning.net/the-evolution-of-spaceship-earth-inc-3/</u> that capitalism and most religions are now almost obsolete; and, given the advent of modern computers, computer programmers, computer software and the internet, it is now technologically feasible to construct a new economic system vastly more efficient, effective and fair than what now exists around Spaceship Earth.

Reading Buckminster Fuller's book Operating Manual for Spaceship Earth *(1969) back in the 1970s stimulated some of these ideas. Fuller was the first writer and thinker I read to assert that computers are the best hope for human survival on Earth, that humans should never do work that machines can do better, and that unemployment can be eliminated overnight by governments issuing mind grants to all citizens, paying them to think.*

Progressives now argue something must be done about poorly regulated quasi-obsolete economic systems, religious systems, legal systems, and production and distribution systems that have resulted in the richest 20 percent of Earthians consuming about 76 percent of all goods and services produced every year on Earth, with the bottom 20 percent consuming about 1.5 percent of all goods and services, while a small free Earthian elite, about 26 million humans own and control about 40 percent of Earth's wealth, living in luxury with almost unlimited options for travel and entertainment, living cheek by jowl among billions of humans mired in poverty, owning almost nothing, doing almost the equivalent of slave labor day in and day out all their lives, yet living in constant fear of being fired from their jobs for disloyalty or slackness, who are condemned to poverty by their wages, in most cases within miles of where they were accidentally born, where they grew up with little or no opportunity to learn relevant knowledge about how the world works, in many cases not even having an opportunity to learn how to read.

I am not advocating abolishing capitalism, communism, socialism, atheism, or any religious ism; since I think certain aspects of capitalism and most religions are humane and beneficial, such as the decentralization of production at the entrepreneurial and small business level and the rewarding of people for creating new ideas, products and services under capitalism. On the other hand, I think the inevitable centralizing of wealth and power in large corporations in the hands of the elite rich caused by capitalism is an incredible abomination, causing many of Earth's most threatening problems, including global warming and inequality among humans, now increasing at a faster rate.

Religions have provided people around Earth solace in the face of grim and gruesome realities of human life, such as inevitable death, and the constant possibility of pain and suffering.

Here's an idea I developed using a management science technique to eventually solve the Earthian poverty and inequality problem, a major cause of today's political and military problems. To my knowledge, I am the first human Earthian to think of this, although I know this is almost impossible, since it's almost impossible for anyone today to think of something that nobody has thought of before. Regardless, I first published this idea in 2008 in my book Business Voyages, *a business bible for people who would like to do the right thing for all Earthians.*

An Earthian *is an individual member of any species of fauna and flora living aboard Spaceship Earth. The human species now threatens the existence of all other species around Earth, and itself, causing hundreds of species to become extinct daily, because of inexorably increasing the human population aboard Spaceship Earth, thereby causing the destruction of habitats and the creating of global warming and climate change, caused by igniting and burning more and more millions of barrels, tons, and cubic feet of oil, coal, and natural gas* every day *, which is necessary to feed, clothe, house, and entertain the burgeoning human population.*

I first read Buckminster Fuller's assertion that the computer would eventually save us in the 1970s in his book titled Operating Manual for Spaceship Earth; *but I, to my knowledge, am the first person to show in some detail how it could happen with computers, computer programming, and the management science technique linear programming. Buckminster Fuller also invented the appellation Spaceship Earth and the word* Earthian.

Here is my schema for how Buckminster Fuller's general idea might come to fruition, from my book Business Voyages, *first published in 2008, from a passage embarking on page 617:*

"It still seems to me Buckminster Fuller in his Operating Manual for Spaceship Earth *(1969) that I first read in 1973 had some of the most creative and cogent ideas I have read for getting humanity out of its ongoing mess. One of Fuller's ideas was that people should not do work that machines can do better. Another of his ideas was that people should be paid to think with mind grants to maintain full employment. Bringing this about in World 1 would require tremendous change, probably entailing decreasing the human population aboard Spaceship Earth through lower birth rates over time, but it seems to me Fuller's ideas about the nature of work, full employment, and prosperity for all could happen, perhaps within the next one hundred years.*

"I do not think any of the economic ideas I have read or heard from Republican or Democratic political candidates in the US in the last year (2003-2004) will do anything to solve problems such as overpopulation in poor countries and jobs being outsourced to poor countries or automated away by robots. Seemingly politicians of all stripes will not or cannot face up to the fact that wages are low in poor countries because there are billions of poor people in such countries willing to work hard for a pittance compared to wages and salaries in rich countries, and so long as such conditions exist workers in rich countries will experience inexorable downward pressure on their wages and salaries because of the iron laws of economic competition and supply and demand, which can only be temporarily suppressed in the short run by politicians bending the laws of economic competition for their favored few through measures such as tariffs, subsidies, currency manipulation, deficit spending, tax reductions, interest rate reductions, and money-printing.

"The long-term solution is for all people aboard Spaceship Earth to get rich, free, and friendly, but to reach that happy state of affairs much patience and sacrifice will be required of billions of poverty-stricken people around the globe—social heroes and martyrs who peacefully live their lives knowing they inherited a relatively mean, short, brutish and unfair fate (Hobbes, 1651).

"Although some biological constructivists think humanity is involved in a meaningless drift in the infinity of time and space, it's possible most people aboard Spaceship Earth could achieve satisfying

lives devoid of economic insecurity and threat of terrorism and military attack within one hundred years. It seems to me this is possible with current rates of progress using free enterprise market systems and democratic political processes, coupled with the ongoing evolutionary bottom-up discovery and application of scientific knowledge (Stapleton & Stapleton, 1998), assuming humans do not blow themselves up with weapons of mass destruction or render themselves extinct with global warming and climate change in the meantime. On the other hand, it's possible that new economic, social, and political alternatives can be tried that might accelerate the current rate of progress; assuming human beings are intelligent enough and creative enough to co-construct them.

"Being a good entrepreneur, or any other kind of good human being, is not easy these days; but despite the gathering storm clouds clearly visible ahead and the wind, heat, and choppy water we are now experiencing caused by religious fanaticism, terrorism, overpopulation, resource depletion, war mongering for profit, and global warming, the entrepreneur remains the captain of his or her ship.

"It is not easy to remain positive and work hard every day running a tight ship dealing with the problems and details of one's particular daily existence while one is constantly reminded by news media that the world is going to hell in a hand basket. While the world may be going to hell in a hand basket at some time, it is not going to self-destruct today, this year, or this decade. Despite the

problems of World 1, there remain myriad opportunities—right now—for entrepreneurs all over Earth to invent, produce, and sell new products, services, and processes, and get rich, as many are doing.

"The problem is that if everyone should ignore global warming, overpopulation, religious fanaticism, energy depletion, unnecessary military activity, and terrorism, focusing solely on her or his personal life problems, goals, and ambitions, problems of global warming, overpopulation, religious fanaticism, resource depletion, terrorism, and war are sure to worsen; and if negative trends caused by these problems continue indefinitely, the "world" could come to an end as prophesied by religious fanatics. To help insure this does not happen, the time may come when all conscientious and intelligent human beings, including self-interested entrepreneurs in the process of getting rich, must contribute a significant portion of their time and money to solving the world's problems if "the world" is to continue to exist.

"Solving problems caused by global warming, religious fanaticism, overpopulation, energy depletion, and terrorism may become the moral equivalent of fighting in world wars, as President Jimmy Carter of the US pointed out regarding the energy crisis of the 1970's, requiring courageous efforts of mythic proportions and the sacrifices of millions of heroes.

"It seems to me a mathematical formulation exists that one day may develop for human Earthians power in economics loosely

analogous to the power of $E=mc^2$ in physics. This formulation is Max or Min C_jX_j, subject to, $A_{ij}X_j \leq$, =, or $\geq B_i$, which is a general form of the linear programming model, which has been around for many years in management science, operations research, and linear algebra courses. It seems to me Max C_jX_j, s.t. $A_{ij}X_j \leq$, =, or $\geq B_i$ symbolizes knowledge that gives the human species about as much potential power to perpetuate itself as $E=mc^2$ symbolizes knowledge that gives the human species the power to exterminate itself.

"The upshot of this linear programming discussion is that if computers and computer programs become powerful enough, they might eventually store data in matrices for food, clothing, shelter, energy, transportation, and medicine requirements for every single human living on Planet Earth. These requirements could be summed to develop the total requirement for food, clothing, shelter, energy, etc. for Earth as a whole, per week, month, year, or whatever. An X_j matrix stored in a magnum computer system might contain all the various products required by humans, a B_i matrix in the linear programming formulation might contain all the types of resources available to produce the required goods, which will constrain production below some limit, an A_{ij} matrix in the LP model might contain the amount of various resources required to produce one unit of each necessity of life, or X_j, and a C_j matrix in the linear programming formulation might contain the relative utility of each alternative good, or X_j.

"The Magnum Computer System could then scientifically compute the optimum number of units of alternative products to produce for humans then alive on Earth, once data have been read into the requisite data bases, by someone clicking an icon energizing a "Do loop" of the magnum program to do the processing of the Magnum Production Schedule. Once the goods are produced the Magnum Computer System could then scientifically distribute them among all humans living on Earth using another quantitative management science technique known as the transportation model to minimize transportation costs from raw materials to finished products to consumers. Such a process would insure the world's resources necessary to sustain human life were used in an optimum manner and were consumed in a generally fair manner.

"Computers can not only store and manipulate data in two dimensional matrices in rows and columns on one plane; they can store and manipulate data in three dimensional matrices that not only go east–west in rows and north–south in columns on one plane, but up and down on different planes. Instead of only having an M x N matrix, you can have an M x N x O matrix, and tell a computer to store data in the cell located at the intersection of the Mth row, the Nth column, and the Oth plane, much like you would park an automobile in a particular space of a multi-story garage. And you can have many more dimensions if you like. You can put M x N x O matrices in larger labeled matrices, and put those labeled matrices in even larger matrices, and so on. Xt,k,c,q,n,p,g, stored in a computer, could be a variable

representing the gth good required by the pth person, in the nth city, of the qth state, of the cth country, of the kth continent, in the tth year, entailing accessing data in 7 interrelated matrices, or dimensions. Subscripts attached to variables such as X in this example tell the computer how to track down specific values through the maze of interrelated matrices. Numbers for the subscripts can theoretically increment from 1 to any finite number (the number of cells in the matrix) and entail that many passes through nested do-loops (7 in this example) in the overall computer algorithm (sequence of iterative mathematical steps) to develop aggregate totals. The process is similar to storing data in labeled files on your personal computer, putting those labeled files in labeled folders, and then putting those labeled folders into other labeled folders, etc., and using subscripts to keep track of what value you put in what variable in what file of what folder.

"Writing a computer program to manage a global economy would require many thousands of man-hours of flowcharting and programming time and a magnum computer system. Requirements for such a project might approximate the man-hour and technical knowledge and skill requirements of the Manhattan project that produced the first atom bomb, or the US space program that put the first man on the moon. Writing such a program would require flowcharting and programming skill many orders of magnitude greater than mine. I have not written a line of computer code since earning my doctorate in 1969, and I learned only one computer language, Fortran IV.

"Using linear programming to schedule world production and distribution of the necessities of life is at present little more than business science fiction, however mathematically feasible this is or shall become as computers and computer software become more powerful and sophisticated. On the other hand, such a system may evolve through time through synergistic learning as more and more humans comprehend what is going on. For more on synergistic learning and comprehension refer back to Buckminster Fuller's definitions of synergy and comprehension in Chapter 1 of Business Voyages, *"Where to Go."*

"It's possible a computerized global economic system shall evolve for the production and distribution of the necessities of life—food, clothing, shelter, and medicine—with the national identities, cultures, political systems, economic systems, religions, and so forth of the some 200 nations now on Earth remaining intact. Free enterprise could exist for everything but the production and distribution of the necessities of life.

I have no idea what are the probabilities of any of these things happening, but it seems to me they are possible, which, it seems to me, is hopeful for all mankind.

"Today in reality the market system, composed of billions of isolated customers voting for the producing of various goods by buying things, is used to decide what to produce and how to distribute the produced items. The market system works adequately for billions of people on Earth, but poorly for a billion or so, those who go to

bed hungry at night. Politicians and bureaucrats spasmodically intervene at various times and places based on impulses, fears, power needs, sympathy, and other motivations to provide charitable aid for fellow humans clearly in need of help, regardless of where the people needing help might have been unlucky enough to have been born on Earth, and regardless of global market determinations, in a loose system of governments and charitable organizations including the United Nations that has enabled the human species as a whole to muddle through.

"Management scientists using something like linear programming to schedule, produce, and distribute the necessities of life for all humanity as outlined above would prove those in control of the Magnum Computer System truly cared about every single human alive on Earth, creating a World 1 in which every man, woman, and child alive on Earth would know for a fact she or he was truly appreciated and protected by a rational fair global system during her or his infinitesimally short existence on Earth. The implementation of such a system might finally untie the Gordian knot that has kept much of mankind threatened and terrorized by fear, ignorance, poverty, hunger, disease, misery and violence since time immemorial."

According to the philosopher Karl Popper, quoted in Business Voyages, "World 1 includes hydrogen and helium, the heavier elements, liquids and crystals, and living organisms; World 2 includes consciousness of self and of death, and sentience or animal consciousness; and World 3 includes works of art and science and technology, human language, and theories of self and of death."

According to Popper and Eccles Worlds 1, 2, and 3 comprise all forms of knowing that humans might discover and construct on Earth, which continually evolve, hopefully at a fast enough rate for humans to learn how to stave off their current existential threats.

To read inside Business Voyages *go to* <u>https:// www.amazon. com/Business-Voyages-Schemata- Discovering-Co-Constructing/ dp/1413480810.</u>

It seems human Earthians must make major changes or live with the probabilities of an environmental catastrophe, possibly extinction. Better birth control measures are needed to reduce overpopulation, a major cause of global warming; and changes must be made in economic strategies and belief systems that inevitably cause Earth's resources to wind up in the hands of fewer and fewer humans who do no work for a living while most of Earth's population becomes poorer and poorer, while the environment is polluted and contaminated more and more, having possibly already passed a tipping point.

Here's an idea for dealing with the over-population problem, which would peacefully shrink Earth's human population from generation to generation until a sustainable population level is reached, by Earthian women deciding to have no more than one child each, of either sex, assuming they had the power to do so.

A solution for the Earthian plight, if there is one, probably entails humans inventing a bottom-up religion and a spiritual god, similar to the god and religion advocated by Michael Adzema and Native American Elders. Adzema defines a spiritual god as the highest moral, ethical, and spiritual state individual humans can achieve, becoming an Atman, using pure subjectivity. Native American elders conceive of god as a Great Spirit that exists in all nature, spiritually present in Earth itself, in its waters, mountains, and animals. These gods are not commanding gods ruling from above, but rather exist in the minds of humans who feel their presence here on Earth.

Native Americans worshipped their ancestors, sensing, feeling and reliving the ego states, beliefs and behaviors that had been introjected into their neuronal networks from earliest childhood, probably even during the perinatal process, from first-hand exposure to mothers in their wombs and their parents and grandparents who showed and used them after birth, which were passed like a baton between runners in a track race every generation since time immemorial, causing the last generation produced to feel, think and do in the here and now much as their ancestors had, which like all human processes on Earth produced both good and bad effects from one perspective or another depending on circumstances.

Both the old God of the Book and the new US surveillance and drone technological god of computers and the internet rely on threats, fear and intimidation to cause humans to do the right thing in the opinion of the gods, using top-down quasi-legal systems with built-in punishments for wrongdoers. The old God also promised a fantastical reward in a heaven throughout eternity as his major incentive for humans who signed up for his program in various religions and who met his expectations and requirements when alive on Earth, and an unspeakable hell throughout eternity for those who did not live up to his expectations and requirements.

One can build the case what humans need now is a non-commanding bottom-up belief system that supports the decisions of all Earthians capable of producing learning that will cause human Earthians to do the right thing for themselves and other species of fauna and flora, causing them to do what is necessary for all to survive and experience a modicum of satisfaction during their infinitesimally short lives, simply because the right thing is the right thing for all species on Earth, with no thought of earning a fantastical eternal reward in some sort of heaven.

The old god fostered economic and legal systems that encouraged the selfish acquisition of land and goods; the new bottom-up god would peacefully encourage the sharing of resources so as to enhance the welfare and survival of all Earthians, not merely the richest, most powerful, most manipulative, most callous, most hypocritical, most deceitful and most obedient.

From a practical standpoint, a program similar to the one above would probably entail the internationalization and amalgamation of all large corporations and industries into one corporation, Spaceship Earth, Inc., so as to produce and distribute the necessities of life in a fair way to all human Earthians. This would entail an overhaul of the way people work and live and their human relationships. In this New World all humans would be born free and empowered; and, like those born truly rich today, they would not have to worry about ever having to work for a living as long as they live.

Under this new regime, every human born on Earth would inherit at birth the same number of stock shares in Spaceship Earth, Inc., which would pay sufficient dividends to provide a decent life year after year until death.

Some jobs in various occupational categories might be impossible to automate, and some humans would have to do those jobs; but greedy humans could be enticed to do those jobs by offering special rewards, if there was no risk of them losing their Spaceship Earth, Inc. dividend check income.

Anyone lucky enough to inherit the right kind of strong, fast, and quick muscles, height, weight, and coordination and a will to win with a willingness to train and work hard could still receive extra rewards by playing sports. The same goes for people lucky enough to inherit artistic and entertainment talents of all sorts. I guess it might be socially acceptable for some of these athletes and entertainers to get filthy rich as they do now, while retaining their Spaceship Earth, Inc. dividend checks, but the main thing would be to make sure every human Earthian had a guaranteed good life provided by their inherited Spaceship Earth, Inc. dividend checks.

This, surely, would finally get rid of the need for large expensive military forces and wars to keep people employed and kill people off.

Most Earthians fully satisfied with their dividend checks from Spaceship Earth, Inc. could spend their time reading, writing and solving math problems, visiting with one another, communicating on the internet, doing scientific experiments, mowing their own grass, perhaps growing some of their own eggs, milk and vegetables, cooking their own food, attending plays and art shows, and traveling now and then on trains and ships powered by green energy to see firsthand new, beautiful and inspiring sights around Earth.

4

BACK DOWN TO EARTH

After about thirty minutes of reading,

Rout–"OK, let's move on. Whoever got hit last spin The Truther."

The Rooster Crowed and The Truther selected George.

George—"As we all know Trump has advocated building a new wall to keep illegal immigrants out of the US from the beginning of his presidency, without much success, I am afraid. The Democratic congress has blocked him in every way on this. On the other hand, some progress has been made. Trump is doing the best job of any president putting America on the right track. I recommend we keep on supporting Trump and make America great again, and forget nonsense about a lunatic fantasy about making the whole world great with something like what this author talks about in this article."

Harrison—"Come on George, you know Trump's idea for a wall was doomed from the start. Seems to me there is less talk of it now than there was, especially with this new influx of immigrants from Central America, but you seem to have forgotten Rout wanted us to discuss the article he assigned. I'm not sure why Rout wanted us to read this fantasy article about Spaceship Earth, but if it did come to pass it would cure immigration problems, since everyone would be paid to stay where they are around earth, which sounds like a good idea to me. On the other hand, the article is worse than socialism, it's a dystopian fantasy showing what great things would happen if artificial intelligence robots took over the management of the entire Earthian economy. Where did you find this article Rout?"

Rout—"I ran across it in an internet journal. I assigned it for reading because the article ties together several aspects of what we have been talking about in our group sessions and it seems to me if it were implemented it would solve most of Earth's problems. I must admit I think there is little chance something like linear programming could ever be used to schedule world production of the necessities of life for all humans, but if it could be it would be a good thing."

Harrison—"Well I suppose in fantasy it might. But how in hell could people ever implement such a thing. As I understand it it would require internationalizing, or taking over, all corporations."

Rout—"No, it would only require taking over corporations directly involved in the production and delivery of the necessities of life. There could be other kinds of corporations in other industries, provided they did not violate resource constraints and requirements for producing the necessities of life.

George—"It'll never happen. It's pure socialism or worse. All freedom would be lost and it would entail redistributing incomes in a major way. In fact it would require a super government confiscating and taking by force all the wealth of existing people. What would you do about housing? How could a billionaire afford to live in a mansion he owns if he has to live off some imaginary dividend check from one corporation, called Spaceship Earth, Inc.? It's crazy. I can't believe you would have forced us to read it, the only time you ever did such a thing. It's becoming clear to me that what you have really wanted to do all along is brainwash us all with socialism or worse pure communism."

Joel—"I'll grant you, the article is a bit radical but it covers a lot of ground and it does make a major point, namely that artificial intelligence and faster and more powerful computers will enable humans to do things that have never been possible before, utilizing data bases that never existed before. And it is based on solid mathematical theory, linear programing, that has been around for a long time. As to its suggestion about the dividend income for all humans, it is similar to MMT, or Modern Monetary Theory. Some experts are advocating paying or giving citizens a basic income to insure there is enough money in circulation to generate a viable economy. And this idea in this article is based on Buckminster Fuller's idea to award mind grants to all Earthian humans to eliminate employment overnight, based on the philosophical notion that all people have value, so paying them to do whatever their talents happened to be might pay off in the long run. It would require massive changes in all countries, not just in the rich countries, but in theory it could work, and something similar to it is probably necessary to stave off global warming and climate change, and human extinction, not to mention the extinctions of many species of fauna and flora around spaceship earth."

Sam—"Very good perspective Joel. Radical changes are going to have to happen, and it's going to require thinkers with more than a little ability to think outside of conventional social, political, religious, and military boxes. Whether a group like Rout's group here can do it remains to be seen. There's a lot of disagreement among the members here. True enough we have learned to respect one another more and I think most of us are more open to differing views and ideas, but I wonder how many of us would vote for something like Spaceship Earth, Inc.

"I would however like to put in my two cents worth about Trump's wall and immigration. I think the whole idea is a paranoid fantasy. Trump's pale-faced followers, a lot of them in any case, obsess about brown-skinned hordes storming across the southern USian border to steal their jobs and take over their great country, you know the country Trump is now making "great" again just for them, when their major threat is AI automation in the US and more and more competition with low wage manual labor workers working all around the world. People don't have to immigrate to the US to steal Trump's follower's jobs; they do it by working in factories built in their own neighborhoods by large US corporations at subsistence wages, thereby setting a worldwide wage rate lower than a living wage for manual labor in the US.

"American history should start with native history, including not only the natives of the USian part of North America but also including the natives of the rest of North America and the natives of Central and South America. Hubristic European-USians are mistaught in families, schools, churches, movies, tv shows, newspapers, and internet memes that they are the only "Americans" aboard Spaceship Earth. All three of the above Earthian continents were cognized and delineated after Amerigo Vespucci landed in what is now known as Central America in 1497, discovering what he called a "New World," after sailing west from Europe to reach the East, specifically India. Hence the natives of the "new world" were thereafter called "Indians." European humans by 1497 had mustered the courage to test the theory that Earth was a globe by sailing on and on in wooden ships farther than the eye could see across the Atlantic Ocean. Amerigo's discovery of a land mass new to Europeans resulted in the extermination in the next few centuries of millions of native inhabitants of all three continents of the new world landed on by Amerigo, who had been there for over a thousand years. It's absurd to think European Earthian humans were the real owners of USian territory in North America and that USian Americans are the only Americans aboard Spaceship Earth. Most European USians are descendants of Europeans who emigrated to North America to get rich or escape dire poverty and religious and ethnic persecution caused by overpopulation in their countries of origin."

Joel—"Give a shout out to the French Revolution of 1789, but cringe about its aftermath. Let us all grieve together that Spaceship Earth today should not evolve and degenerate similarly. Let us grieve that any USian president does not become another Napoleon Bonaparte. It seems to me Earthian humans need no more republic democracies. They need real democracies."

Rout—"It is becoming clearer to the donors and others privy to the tapes and videos of the group sessions that feelings, thoughts, beliefs, and behaviors in this group are changing for the better. You are becoming more comfortable and relaxed and are less fearful about honestly saying what you think in the discussions. OKness levels have increased.

"OKness is a major concept in the transactional analysis literature, the whole discipline being based on simple colloquial terms that could be used to discuss relatively complex problems, issues, and states of affairs. Of the psychological, social, economic, and psychological disciplines I have studied, it seems to me transactional analysis is the most helpful in understanding system dynamics by providing simple language anyone can use to discuss complex psychological issues. Not only is it concerned about increasing OKness in organizations and groups; it provides specific tools for assessing different kinds of OKness. All organizations and groups are relatively OK or not OK depending on circumstances, OK with respect to themselves, other individuals, other groups, and the world, or universe. How individuals, groups, and organizations came to be caused to wind up at their level of OKness is a relevant question. A deeper relevant question is whether individuals, organizations, and groups are caused to be what they are in terms of OKness or whether they are just pretending to be OK at those levels? As with all social and psychological phenomena a major question is whether perceived feelings, thoughts, behaviors, and decisions are real or faked. Are perceived feelings, thoughts, and behaviors naturally caused to exist or are they constructions created to simulate natural feelings, thoughts, decisions, behaviors, and the like?

"Fritz Perls, the founder of Gestalt therapy, used to say, "Most talking is a lie," meaning he thought most people were rarely truthful about what they were actually feeling, thinking, and doing. Perls called most ordinary conversation chickenshit, most organizational communication bullshit, and most philosophical discussions elephantshit. He thought humans are rarely truly honest about what they feel, think, and do about things because of their vested interests and ulterior motives. In most organizations and groups people are rewarded not only with strokes but money for conforming to the requirements of the authority structure of the organization. One can build the case that almost no one can be fully honest in organizations and groups, that most humans appear as they do after having manipulated themselves through various adaptations to conform to organizational scripts imposed at their level and position in the organizational hierarchy to hold their jobs.

"To paraphrase Upton Sinclair, a muckraking USian novelist and socialist politician, "It's difficult to convince people of the real truth of something when their livelihoods depend on not believing it." So, it's not easy to tell by looking just how OK a person, group, or organization really is. One can observe in groups and organizations how time is being structured, by noting what people are doing. TA has five categories for describing time structuring: withdrawal, pastimes, rituals, work, Games, and intimacy. Withdrawal means people are not engaged with others or groups, withdrawing in their heads or physically removing themselves from others. One can tell by looking whether individuals are tuning others out, daydreaming, etc.

"In this group The Truther precludes withdrawal and pastiming, chit-chatting about the weather, talking about hobbies and sports, or interests in children, cooking, and the like. The Truther and the De-Gaming rules require members to do some intellectual work, such as define problems, figure out alternatives for dealing with problems, and figure out what to do about problems and opportunities. There are almost no rituals in this Game-free process, no reciting of routine platitudes, dogmas or doctrines, or housekeeping duties, such as voting on past business. No yak-yakking, yuk-yukking, or gee-hawing. Games are outlawed by The Truther and the group rules. No one can legitimately say they have been Rescued, Persecuted, or Victimized when The Truther selects them. Intimacy is also precluded during the group sessions, depending on the type of intimacy one is talking about. Talk about sexual intimacy is not allowed, but talk about facts of states of affairs is supposed to be true, a prerequisite for intimacy. In general intimacy involves telling the truth about what one feels, thinks, decides, and does. In this sense one can build the case a major objective of this group to increase time spent in intimacy and decrease time spent in other types of time structuring, such as withdrawal, pastiming (what most humans call bullshitting), and Game-playing, which are observable phenomena, which seems to have already happened in this group.

"Watching the videos of the group sessions and listening to the tapes it's possible for observers to notice changes in these phenomena. Other things that can be observed are Parent, Adult, and Child transactions within the group. Transactions are communication vectors beamed between one ego state in one individual to one ego state in another in pair stimulus-response vectors. There are three types of ego states, Parent, Adult, and Child. Ego states are emotional and behavioral states of being that appear parent-like, adult-like, and child-like. Individuals, groups, and organizations transmit messages to others in various combinations, and individuals and groups respond in certain ways to what has been transmitted to them using various combinations of ego states. The Truther cathects (a TA word for activating or turning on ego states) Adult ego states. Parent and Child ego states can also be seen at times in the group by noting facial expressions and body language. Parent ego states usually entail dogmatic statements and stern facial expressions and pointed index fingers used for emphasizing the person is in a Parent ego state and should be listened to by others after they dutifully cathect their Adapted Child Ego states. It has become obvious to me and the board of advisors that the process has increased the use of the Adult ego state in the group and has increased honesty or intimacy within the group. Whether this improvement will transfer to other groups the members of this group belong to remains to be seen.

"Here's the hard part. You can have good OK groups and organizations but still have not have not-OK governments and economic systems. If not-OK people get in control of organizations, regardless of the type of economic system they use, the organization will not produce OKness for everyone. Such is now the case with capitalism, which is producing massive inequality with the rich getting richer while the rest stagnate or decline, while governments do and say things to make lower and middle classes feel, think, and believe they are more OK than they really are. One way to do that is by starting wars, which takes the minds of not-OK people off their economic plights and puts them to work fighting wars.

"An issue is how much longer we should continue this Group. One can build the case The Group has already proved it can produce increases in human OKness. Would continuing the process for more months or years eventually result in creating consensual answers for society and psychological problems. Most likely it would, but the problem as always is not only to produce consensual answers but to implement them to make every one more OK. There have always been major differences among the OK levels of humans. A purpose of religion has been to cause people to think they are OK regardless of their actual psychological, social, economic, and political life positions.

"TA organizational and group analysis is concerned with agitations and cohesions among leaders and members in and among organizations. To fully analyze organizations and groups you need to find out not only whether members are OK but how agitated or cohesive they are at various boundaries of the organization, internal and external, and whether the agitations and cohesions are between members or between members and leaders, there being three general types of leaders—designated, psychological, and effective. Once such agitations are located various and sundry consensual answers might be developed to deal with them."

"Spaceship Earth is now experiencing increased agitations, between leaders and members within organizations and groups and between organizations and groups, including agitations between leaders of nations and their own group members, and between some two hundred nations around Spaceship Earth. It appears the root causes of the increased agitations are economic policies and new technologies, which are causing global warming, climate change, and income inequality. No amount of organizational and group therapy will cure these problems unless humans can get Earthian humans together to discuss how to create new economic systems and technologies to solve the real causes of the agitations.

"Spaceship Earth is also now experiencing negative feedback loops that exacerbate the conflict and agitations. Relatively agitated not-OK voters in so-called democracies vote for not-OK individuals as leaders because the leaders reinforce followers' not-OKness, leading to even more not-OK policies and behavior. Burning more and more fossil fuel necessary to produce more economic growth to feed, clothe, and house larger and larger numbers of fecund Earthian humans alive on Earth leads to increased global warming causing more and more polar ice to melt causing more and more methane gas to be released leading to more global warming and so on. How to resolve the whole problem before it's too late entails comprehending whole systems, not just parts of systems. What's good for a part often harms the whole. The fallacy of composition is rampant in Earthian economic states of affairs."

SESSION FOUR
SEATTLE, WASHINGTON
JANUARY 2020

The Truther Rooster Selected Tony.

"God, I can't believe I finally got hit by that thing. I have spent a lot of my life behind a bar, listening to people carry on about their lives and beliefs, and now I get to do it before this group. Well, to cut to the chase, with no bullshit,

I think it's all bullshit. Most people don't know crap about what is going on. They run their mouths about what makes them feel a little better. They've all got their beliefs, friends, mommas and daddies, kids, and that sort of thing, and their girlfriends and wives and husbands and boyfriends and that sort of thing. Many of them are very critical about how things have turned out and have some sort of idea about what they think should be done to do to make things better. A lot of them hate socialism and politics. Some of them hate capitalism. Some hate liberals. Some hate conservatives. I listen to them and do what I can to make them feel better, standing behind a bar. A shot of whiskey or a beer will help, and I try to keep them resupplied when they run dry. That's the way I make my living, for god's sake. The bottom line is that most people don't know shit about what's going on. How to cure that is a major problem. It's as if they aint learned nothin' all their lives. Whose fault is that? Their parents? Their teachers? Their preachers? If they had any. A lot of them are just sittin' at a bar killing' time the best way they know how. Alcohol is a good sedative, you know. Does it make their lives better or worse? I think overall better. You know Karl Marx called religion the opium of the people. The fact is a lot of people need alcohol, drugs, and shit to get through the day. That's why I'm there, behind the bar. What do I recommend? Just keep pourin' out that rot gut doin' my job. It's better than diggin' ditches. Tellin' people what to do about Spaceship Earth is way beyond my pay grade."

Joan—"I think you're right, Tony. About all most people can do is do their job, however they happened to wind up in it, if they are lucky enough to have one, as best they can to make a living. I suppose you bartenders must be a little more sympathetic than most people. I have leaned on a few myself. I don't think bars and bartenders are going away anytime soon. They may be getting more necessary as time goes by. Good for you. I'll bet you're a good bartender."

Wendell—"I like to have a beer myself sitting at a bar now and then. I would hate to think there weren't any bars around. I used to hang out in some of them quite a bit before I got married, but I have not done much of it for quite a while. I'm so tired at night now about all I can do is sit down at the table to eat what the wife has fixed for supper. After plodding around on a farm, doing all sorts of jobs, sometimes ten or twelve hours, you don't need a beer or a shot of whiskey. All you need is some food and a good night's sleep for the next day. My wife and I still go into town now and then and live it up a little with a few drinks and some good food she did not have to cook at home. I don't think the problem in this country is alcohol or people hanging out in bars. The problem is politicians doing almost nothing but hanging out in bars and restaurants bullshitting with cronies, lobbyists, and such, trying to cut deals for campaign financing. About all they care about is getting more money for their next election. As I understand it the bar business has done well in the past few years and has done relatively well compared to most businesses, one of the kinds of businesses that has done well, hiring workers, not laying them off. The farm economy is a mixed bag. On the one hand, you have the corporate farmers and the big sole proprietor farmers who have made a little money. But most small family farmers have had a tough time of it. They all hire the same cheap labor from Central and South America to do as much of the stoop labor as possible, but the main thing now is using these new expensive humongous tractors and harvesting machines and chemical herbicides and fertilizers. There is almost no way a small family farmer can compete with a corporation. He can't get his hands on enough land to justify taking out loans and pay interest to banks required to buy tractors and equipment required to farm with a decent profit at that scale. It's a bleak situation for the small family farmer. Hell, I would not blame any of them for hanging out in bars more than they do, if they could afford it."

Albert—"I also like to have a drink now and then in a bar. There's a certain nostalgia about it. Relaxing. Like you can just let it all hang out for a while if you can bring along someone or find anyone interesting to talk with. We physicists have it easy in some ways, assuming we can find a job with a decent salary. All we need do is think about things that can be proved certain and tested in various ways. This economic and political stuff, though, especially this psychological stuff is something else. Nothing it seems to me can be proved true in economics, psychology, or politics with data and mathematics or a laboratory experiment. But it's obvious to me some of you guys in here know more about it than most people because of your education, experience, and training. In physics you are an expert only if you can prove what you are talking about is true with data and mathematics in some sort of experiment or test. Seems to me in economics, psychology, politics, and the like an expert is just someone who because of education and experience should know more about it than others. Either way it's not an easy life. Most physicists live their lives without ever achieving any sort of recognition as a physicist because of never encountering or discovering anything new in the real world that he or she can prove true for the first time. Albert Einstein was a rare exception for a physicist. In the worlds of economics, politics, religion, and society there are so many charlatans out there almost nothing can be proved true, and few of them can be trusted to tell what they really think the truth is even if they know what the truth is. Probably most are them just brown-nosers and ass-kissers. A lying fool like Trump gets a thousand times more recognition in one day than most physicists get in their lives. It's a wonder bars do not stay busier than they do, as crazy as the so-called real world really is."

Mikhail—"I agree with you Albert. I have been a CPA for a long time. I have made a decent living and I enjoy helping my clients. But I assure you you are never going to get rich and famous doing what real accountants are supposed to do, tell the truth, the whole truth and nothing but the truth about true states of affairs of people and businesses, using double-entry bookkeeping. Harry Truman once said there is no way you can get rich as a politician if you are not a crook. The same thing is true for the accounting profession, if you are doing real accounting work. True enough you might get moderately rich if you become the lead partner in a very large firm, in which case you are not getting rich doing accounting work but taking a cut from the revenue generated by accounting work done by many other accountants under you. No, the only way you can get filthy rich under capitalism is to be born rich or get monopoly control of something like the MS-DOS operating system like Bill Gates did or cream the stock market like Elon Musk did with electric cars and spaceships feeding off revenue generated by thousands of underlings and selling off your founder's stock, or just by getting lucky taking wild-assed guesses in some sort of stock, bond, or commodities market, or maybe something like bitcoins. There is a company or two out there in which the founders have gotten filthy rich programming supercomputers with AI programs based on historical frequencies and observed correlations within and between markets to automatically make trades in markets that have gotten filthy rich. So, yeah, we need a lot of bars in which to talk this over. It does bother my ass that a nit-wit like Donald Trump can get all the attention and recognition he gets by telling lies and making simple stupid off-the-wall comments. Why should he be rich and famous when millions of smarter hard-working people never even come close to getting rich and famous doing their jobs?"

Rout—"Well, I have got to put in my own two-cents worth here. I could not agree more with what has been said here. Yes, of course, only a few not necessarily very bright people are taking all the glory for achievements of the USian economy. Why is this happening? It's happening because that's the way it has always happened, no matter the economic or political system, but it's worse now because of the megaphone nature of modern communications technology. Only a few humans can get on television and in mass media, and most people don't even want to. They enjoy their private lives, if they can get their needs met in decent jobs and professions. Why make a fool of yourself strutting around in public making inane simple-minded inflammatory statements getting recognized for doing nothing like Trump does? Yet it happens all the time. A lot of people are hungry for recognition, but most are like frogs in a pond, sitting on a lily pad, croaking, but being ignored. On the other hand, a lot of people are ego-maniacs like Trump.

"What is recognized and prized by the USian government? Just look at the Federal budget. What is being paid for with public money, both real money taken in in the form of taxes and funny money taken in in the form of Treasury bill and note sales, made to the Federal Reserve and others. Over fifty percent of the USian discretionary budget is now paid out to the USian military-industrial complex, almost one trillion dollars per year, many more times more per year than any other item of the budget, such as welfare, education, the environment, etc. Who has received the most recognition throughout USian history? A few military generals and politicians. The mass of people that made USian history happen could not be mentioned. That's the way it always is. Only a few glory hounds get mentioned in the history books.

"As you know, the worst problems Spaceship Earth faces right now are global warming and climate change and the Earthian money and banking system. Experts say global warming can cause mass extinctions in decades, maybe even *homo sapiens,* and it is obvious the Earthian money and banking system could collapse because of flooding the system with funny money, not only in the US, but in all Earthian economies, creating debts than cannot be repaid with real money, requiring more and more funny money to be created from thin air by central banks every year by simply punching digits into computers and calling the resulting numbers money to keep kicking the can down the road and keep on making the payrolls of militaries, military contractors, and military suppliers making guns, bullets, tanks, airplanes, rockets, nuclear bombs, ships, etc. If these military-derived payrolls are not made a depression will immediately occur with untold millions of Earthian humans thrown out of work, however little recognition they are receiving for the work they do now, which is at root basically a busywork system. If all countries profess to be defending themselves from others building up their economies with military industrial complex work then most of them can appear to be almost fully employed with their politicians appearing to be doing a good job deserving to stay in power. If all of them should suddenly declare peace against one another the entire Earthian economic system would collapse with billions unemployed with mass starvation, so we have perpetual war aboard Spaceship Earth and more and more global warming caused by fueling the system that requires more and more economic growth, and nobody knows how to change the system."

Ron—"As some of you know, I drive trucks. I have sat in here as long as I can without sayin' nothin'. The Truther never seems to point me out, but I am gonna say something right now come hell or high water. Where did this recognition crap come from? Whoever said you were supposed to get recognized for doin' your job. How about us truck drivers? We almost never get recognized for anything. But I'll tell you one thing: we sure as hell aint doin' busywork. If we stopped haulin' shit around, food and whatnot, millions of people would start starvin' to death damn quick. About the only recognition we ever get is gettin' one more paycheck, and not gettin' fired that week. And you aint gonna get rich drivin' trucks."

Rout—"I agree completely, Ron, that truck drivers are unsung heroes in the USian economy doing one of the most necessary jobs out there. But unfortunately, the situation is unlikely to change much anytime soon. One can build a case no job in a truly free enterprise economy with competitive free markets is a busywork job, since no purely selfish profit-maximizing consumer or employer is going to pay any more than is necessary for anything; but the reality is such a condition has never existed for all people in all countries. Soldiers, weapons manufacturers, preachers, teachers, politicians, and government workers in all countries have never had to sell themselves in truly free enterprise markets. Prices are set by agreements of various sorts, not by competitive bidding, in many cases, creating distortions of what might have been free enterprise market prices. We now have such distortions in spades in major markets such as the stock market, the housing market, and money markets, thanks to central banks in all countries, including the USian Federal Reserve System arbitrarily increasing prices increasing prices by pumping funny money into the system, in many cases buying assets to manipulate market prices. Military industrial complexes have never been fully subjected to competitive market pricing.

Nobody knows for sure how the USian Pentagon determines prices for people and things they buy, not being subject to the rigors of competitive markets.

"With respect to the notion that all military industrial complexes in all countries are engaged in a form of busywork, it is busywork in the sense that if all countries were to declare peace against one another there would be no need for the goods and services military industrial complexes produce. One can build a case however that Earthian governments have colluded and lied by saying they have to spend and do what they do militarily to protect their people, when it may be the real reason they are doing it is to build up their economies and keep their politicians in power. Regardless, if some force could convince all Earthian governments there is no need for war and war-making jobs they could all send all their war-makers home and pay them for doing nothing and be better off monetarily because of cost savings in energy, transportation, and maintenance.

Spaceship Earth would become better off because of reductions in global warming caused by burning less fossil fuel, not to mention improvements in the quality of human life caused by reductions in human suffering, misery, and premature deaths. So-called defense industries and militaries are now among the greatest producers of global warming around Spaceship Earth, burning more fossil fuel than anybody else. Perhaps a better term for them might be offense industries.

"With respect to the notion that no politician can get rich unless he's a crook, one can build a case no one can get rich quick starting from scratch doing anything unless he or she is a crook of sorts. Since no one can produce enough personally doing anything to get rich quick the only way anyone can get rich in a hurry is to get in control of the lives of others in such a way as to take a cut of what they produce. The top six executives at Wal-Mart can get rich in one year by getting paid $116,000,000 million, garnered by taking a $116 cut from a million employees below them in the chain of command, not by producing that much personally. That's the secret of capitalism itself of course.

"On the other hand, that's peanuts compared to Elon Musk with his self-driving cars, solar panels, batteries, and space ships, who became the richest man aboard Spaceship Earth by age fifty, starting from scratch with a physics degree and an economics degree, who got paid one way or the other one year by the high-tech corporations he started and controlled almost four hundred thousand dollars a day, the most of any executive in Earthian history. Musk, for sure, is highly successful doing what good entrepreneurs do under capitalism. He's maybe the most successful entrepreneur in Earthian history."

SESSION FIVE
FEBRUARY 2020
DALLAS, TEXAS

The Truther rooster Selected Martin

Martin— "Here we are in the Heart of Texas, or should I say in the heart of Texas traffic. I don't think I have ever seen such a tangled mess of traffic in my life, cloverleaf intersections and entrances and exits everywhere. I'm lucky I took a cab in from the airport. I can't imagine how anyone could ever learn to get around in this mess of highway mazes. I never realized Dallas was as large a city as it is. I lived and worked here for a few months in 1962. It's hard to believe how much the place has changed. On the other hand, once you get into the hotel, it's like we're home again. One central city hotel is about like another.

"As a religious studies professor it seems to me the biggest problem right now is people not having a firm set of anything they can believe in, something to put their faith in, not knowing whether there really is a god, and if so, what kind of god. It seems to me the alternative prescriptions are all authoritarian, dogmatic and doctrinaire, telling people not to question what the bible says. On the other hand, can humans develop some sort of non-authoritarian god , a non-anthropomorphic god, with no human characteristics, that does not care for anyone personally or human relationships, who merely creates certain scientific principles and phenomena, such as what we can see, hear, and feel in the physical world, the verifiable world of cause and effect, somewhat akin to the great spirit of native peoples on north America, as mentioned in that article Rout made us read during our last session.

"It seems to me this is what is most akin to what is really going on. I have not seen one scintilla of evidence with my own eyes that any sort of god has ever told anyone to do anything or who has ever done anything because of having been asked to do something in any sort of prayer. Thus, there is no way to have any sort of human-like relationship with any sort of god. On the other hand, one can believe in and have faith in the laws of nature.

"This kind of god created by humans themselves would simply be a human spirit that infuses humans with confidence and courage, and an ability to see reality for what it is. This god is somewhat like what was recommended in 'The Evolution of Spaceship Earth, Inc.' This is what I recommend today, that humans evolve such a god and spirit and forget about heaven and hell and dogma and doctrine and authoritarian threats."

Ellen—"I am inclined to agree with you, Martin. On the other hand, I do not believe most people would take this view. Most people have been so ingrained with authoritarian religious notions and threats of everlasting hells and such, and even physical punishment on earth, such as beheadings, floggings, and stoning's, and other barbaric punishments that they would never go along with this. Some people even remember that humans were burned at the stake for not believing certain religious dogmas and doctrines not too many years ago."

Margaret—"As a civil servant for the government I can tell you in our current political culture you had better keep your mouth shut about such things when at work and at most places or you can damage your career. You might not get fired for talking about such things but you can be punished in other ways, not promoted, or not given decent raises. The best thing to do about religion is not say anything about it in public."

Clarence—"Being a lawyer it's interesting to me how religious people especially evangelicals keep trying to cram religious oriented laws down the throats of people, even the idea that there should not be separation of church and state. There are those in the US who are just like the Taliban in Afghanistan, who want to turn the US into a religious theocracy of some sort. There are those who think that god should actually run the country. Remember Bush II telling us god told him to invade Iraq? We have had presidents in recent decades, such as Bush who told the USian people that they did things like start major wars because a god told them to. Now this is very problematic. Did Bush II actually hear a voice in his head that he really thought was god who told him to go to war? I doubt it. Was he lying about this? Most likely but who could prove it? The problem is nothing about a god can be proved, and consequently manipulators and despots can use the notion of god to manipulate people at will, which is lying of the worst kind, but there is nothing anyone can do about it. Trump does this sort of thing all the time, even participating in religious rituals with a sanctimonious look on his face, and later saying to others in private he thought it was pure bullshit."

Napoleon—"It's like the don't ask don't tell policy in the military. Just pretend it does not exist. Even if you believe it does. There ain't no way in hell to win that war. People have been fighting wars over religion forever and nobody has ever won one yet. Some religions still have a lot of power. True enough there are more nonbelievers percentage wise than there used to be. I'm not sure about the numbers on this but I am pretty sure most people are not as brainwashed by religion as they used to be. My namesake, the real Napoleon, said religions are here to keep the poor from killing the rich."

George—"There is no way you can win an election in the US today if you do not pretend to believe in a god, without saying things like god bless you and god bless America and such. Bush II is a good example. He got religion here in Texas when he lost an election for a minor post, and vowed he would never get out-Christianed again. That's why he started hearing a god talking to him in his head, maybe after he gave up drinking. When you get right down to it religions are like political parties. People, some people at least, are so fearful of what will happen to them after they die that they will pay money to preachers to save them from hell, and some are so greedy that they will sell their souls on earth to get a better seat in heaven, but most in my opinion join religious organizations to gain political power and support in their communities to satisfy their own selfish day in and day out needs, to get more customers for their business, or to make sure they are not marginalized or punished in some way in their communities. Joining a church makes people feel more secure, especially politicians, in their daily lives and careers, not only in their presumed afterlives."

Luke—"I've put up with this as long as I can. I sold my soul to the devil for five thousand dollars a month to come to these meetings and hear the blasphemy I've heard, and I have tried to keep my mouth shut, knowing full well it was hopeless trying to convince you sinners of the error of your ways. I am now convinced this group is the work of the devil, a plot of Satan conceived in the very bowels of hell, where you people, or at least most of you, most assuredly deserve to go. I have tried to pray for you and your immortal souls, but I am losing my patience. You are damned for questioning and criticizing the holy word of the Lord."

Julia—"I wish we didn't talk about this. It makes me sick to my stomach."

Joel—"I wish we didn't too, but we have to. Who can sit back and watch and listen to what is happening to our world and not say something about what one thinks is the truth of the matter? For sure some of the most serious hatreds and problems including wars are still being caused by or partly caused by religions and religious beliefs, dogmas, and doctrines. What is the major cause of war? I think the main cause is simply a lust for power and arrogance. People not only want to possess power but they want to have the ability to tell others what to do, bullies fighting other bullies just for the fun of it, but the next major cause of war is poverty, too few resources poorly distributed to satisfy needs, so one group or organization or country is always trying to steal resources from others somewhere around Earth. It's built in to society, but religion is a factor since it enables people to get power, as has been discussed in this group. What is the solution? Outlaw religions? Communist Russia tried that. Look at what happened to them. They not got poorer and poorer economically while they got politically more powerful developing nuclear bombs and military might, but they wound up getting rid of not only communism but atheism. Putin and Russia are now as hypocritical about religion as were the Russian czars. The place now appears to believe again in capitalism run by Putin as a military dictatorship and oligarchy for the rich, using their longtime orthodox Christian religion much the same as hereditary Russian czars did to manipulate and exploit serfs before the Russian Revolution of 1917. US governments now try to make Russia out to be a serious threat to the US to justify military spending, which they are because of their six thousand or so nuclear bombs manufactured during their communist days, but economically they are little more than a third world country, with a GNP about one-tenth the size of the US's. They are not a real threat at all. It's all bullshit. Putin is more a public relations man than anything else spinning and manipulating shit to make Russia look great again."

Joan—"As you know I work for an insurance company and I can tell you religion is not something you want to talk about at work in a large insurance company. In fact, you don't want to talk about anything but how to do your job. Most people who work for a living do not have time to think about religion. It is not only irrelevant it is unproductive. It saps the productive energy of workers. One fringe benefit to having a good job like I have is that you do not have time for or any responsibility for even thinking about religion. You are free of it at work. I think all people should be."

SESSION SIX
MINNEAPOLIS, MINNESOTA
MARCH 2020

Should Rout start writing some sort of book or report for the donors now letting them know what had transpired? It was not easy keeping track of all the common threads in the discussions in terms of content, but it was even more difficult to accurately note and assess the changes that had occurred in the personalities of the group members. The group had become more cohesive and more Game-free and it appeared some of them were now enjoying participating in the discussions rather than just going through the motions.

It was now clear the new Corona virus, Covid-19, was a real and serious threat and The Group would have to cease operating in its current face-to-face format. Rout however decided not to open this for discussion in this session if no one else wanted to talk about it. He would let the group members know what he and the donors had decided to do about this later in the month of March.

The Truther rooster selected Marshall.

Marshall—" Well, being a weatherman, it seems to me the biggest problem today is climate change, caused by human-caused global warming, burning too much fossil fuel. As you know there are no easy answers. But probably the major problem is that most humans have not accepted the fact that human-caused climate change has happened.

"Personally, I think it goes back to the religion problem. Quite simply it seems to me most people believe a god will solve all their problems regarding the environment, or they just don't give a rip because they think they are going to heaven after they die. They do not believe the problem has to be managed by humans. They believe since a god is all powerful, he must want the climate to be the way it is, since he created the earth and everything in it, including the climate. And to some extent they're right. What power does the average person have to affect the climate? Absolutely none acting alone, but if all humans, all seven plus billion of them now on Earth, collectively seriously discussed the problem they might decide to help correct the problem by doing simple things like driving cars less or changing their diets to consume less food produced by processes requiring fossil fuel.

"Factory agriculture is a problem. It requires using automated machinery and chemicals instead of human energy to plant and grow crops, machinery requiring the burning of fossil fuel as an energy source and instead of controlling weeds and insects by human energy chemical fertilizers are used, many of which are chemically derived from fossil fuel.

"I watched the town hall meeting last night and listened to the democratic candidates giving their opinions on climate change. I was surprised that most of them agreed that climate change is real and is a threat. Some of them hammered the point home that humans only have about eleven years before it will be too late to prevent catastrophic consequences, possibly extinction. Some agreed that fossil fuel emissions must be reduced by fifty percent by 2050.

"As several of them pointed out hundreds of Earthian species are being rendered extinct right now, largely caused by increases in human population. The human population has about doubled in the last fifty years requiring quantum increases in resources to produce and house them. If the human population should double again in the next fifty years this alone could cause human extinction and the extinction of most other species on earth, largely because of habitat destruction necessary to produce enough food to feed fourteen billion humans aboard Spaceship Earth.

"As some of the candidates pointed out humans need to start thinking more about Spaceship Earth and worry less about their nations getting more than its share of Earthian resources. Selfishly pursuing your own interests as an individual or as a group, especially as a member of a large nation, could cause human extinction. Selfishness is a major problem. Humans have got to think more altruistically and benevolently or else the end is nigh, or so it seems to me.

"How to get humans to do this it seems to me is a major problem. This sort of change will require changing not only economic systems and but religious and political systems. The pure capitalistic economic system is basically obsolete. How to shift from what we have now to a viable and sustainable economic system is perhaps the greatest problem.

"Quite naturally this is going to require cooperation between nations and much less competition. I agree with the author of the Evolution of Spaceship Earth that this is the way to go. I'm not sure however whether we have enough time left for this sort of evolution to naturally occur and correct the problem.

Hal—"I was afraid Trump would pour more Federal Reserve system funny money and real tax money into the world's biggest busywork socialistic non-market system, the USian military industrial complex, some say a necessary evil generating untold millions of socialistic non-competitive non-market jobs around Spaceship Earth, yet a major cause of the USian budget deficit and debt, and there are no verifiable serious military threats to the US around Spaceship Earth. Trump has given the military more money than they asked for, but he has not started any new major wars. Talk about negative feedback loops, the US uses the USian military to build up employment not only in the military itself but also among so-called defense industry contractors making airplanes, tanks, ships, and what have you, that consumes more fossil fuel than anything else exacerbating the whole global warming thing melting the polar ice caps and all that. It seems as if the USian government has decided that waging peace aboard Spaceship Earth is more dangerous for the USian economy and society than fostering and waging war. In effect the deep state and the powers that be have decided USians cannot afford peace, a luxury item, so they foster and wage unending war, causing more and more competition and conflict, not cooperation, among nations aboard Spaceship Earth."

John—"It might be feasible to write computer code to use something like linear programming as suggested in the Evolution of Spaceship Earth, that Rout had us read back in the Asheville meeting, but how could you possibly make the required political, religious, and military changes. In all organizations the biggest problem is not writing computer code to make the organization more efficient but resistance on the part of managers and others who do not want their personal power and perks to be reduced by more efficient and effective computer programming. If you look at this problem within and among countries the problem is horrendous. Can you imagine getting heads of all corporations worldwide and current stockholders within corporations worldwide to consent to turn over their power and perks to computer programmers who would write computer code to determine what Earthian resources would be used to produce and distribute the necessities of life to all Earthian humans in an optimum calculation, including using clean green energy sources instead of fossil fuel. It would require a massive redistribution of wealth the likes of which has never been seen on Earth before, including a redistribution of wealth from the USian military to Earthian civilians."

Socrates—"Right on John. People have a will to power and having power is what makes the world go round. You can build a case if you were to cut the power of people to this extent it would cause widespread depression, loss of self-esteem, life satisfaction, and whatnot. What good would life be if there was nothing to work for? If all you had to do every day was sit around and wait for your dividend check to get deposited in your bank account what sort of purpose in life would be this be? People need to work and suffer to feel like they are useful. In effect there would be no purpose for humans if they had peace. Relative to the computer artificial intelligence system they would be worse off than children relative to their parents in terms of dependence, or manual workers, serfs, or slaves relative to landowners and masters in factories. Buckminster Fuller's notion that humans should never do work machines can do better is one of the most dangerous propositions I have ever heard of. At least give folks make work jobs to stay busy, such as the US military."

Sam—"Yes, but what option do we have but to at least try to bring something of this nature about? I assure you I will continue to write articles advocating this sort of thing, The problem though is how do you get people to read such articles? One of the major problems right now is that there is so much information out there from so many different sources on the internet that no can possibly absorb it all. How can anyone have any impact as an individual. The National Security Administration right now can capture just about any human transmission that is made electronically, emails, internet posts, and what have you. They have a fenced-off secure datacenter out in the Utah desert containing over one million square feet of space stocked with servers capable of storing gadzillions of electronic transmissions daily from all kinds of electronic devices used by all humans, consuming god knows how much electrical energy, causing the burning of no telling how much fossil fuel to generate the electricity. But even using computers and AI algorithms they have no way of sifting through this humongous daily inflow and pile of data to screen out relevant data to prevent disasters such as 9/11. Meanwhile, most writers and social activists are preaching to their own choirs, in various media with low numbers of eyeballs attracted, using limited data bases, not really knowing what is going on in the whole system, not saying anything likely to produce significant change."

Barbara—"As a housewife I feel like a fish out of water here but I will say something. Most of you people are far more qualified than I am to say things in thus group. But what difference does it make if you are qualified or not. Nobody knows anything for sure. When I am not taking care of my kids or doing chores around the house I do sometimes listen to the news and learn a little about what you are talking about here. I have no idea what linear programming is and I know nothing about computer programming. I have no idea how it's done. But I can tell you most of what you are talking about here would never be mentioned on the tv programs I watch. Most people like me are totally shut off from these kinds of questions and issues. I can't imagine how anyone like me could possibly be of any value in working these sorts of problems out. Why would you want to pay me five thousand dollars a day to just sit here and listen and say something about something I have no idea about is beyond me, but so long as you keep on payin' out the money, I have no choice but to keep on comin' to these meetings. I need the money for my family."

Joel—"I'm with you Barbara, except I am a university professor, not a housewife, a professor of economics, and I can assure you I am not qualified to write computer programs using linear programming or depose corporate chief executives or convince politicians we need a new economic system. But I can say something about class structures which are relevant here. As Karl Marx pointed out most economic activity is class based, and classes evolved from high to low with a hierarchy and various levels of well-being, prestige, and power. It seems to me so far in history class structures have never been eradicated in societies. This Spaceship Earth idea involves a basically classless society, one class of shareholders in a giant monolithic corporation, owning one share of stock, who receive all their necessities of life paid for by dividends on their one share of ownership stock. They in effect own Spaceship Earth, which if it were to be implemented today, would entail about seven and one half billion stockholders. On the other hand, this system would allow humans to do other things on their own in small businesses and careers for additional money and rewards, based on their inherited abilities, whether artistic, athletic, or whatever, or do mundane service jobs for extra money if they wished. In this sense there would still be a status hierarchy in such a society. How you would regulate the winners in this process to prevent what the winners do now by exploiting the less fortunate I do not know. Would the AI computer system somehow do this? Some people are now afraid AI robots could become so much more intelligent than humans that they would rule the roost at the top of the status hierarchy, and possibly decide to exterminate some or all humans. If AI robots and computer programs should develop general intelligence that exceeds human general intelligence as much as computer accuracy and speed doing mathematical calculations now exceeds human capabilities, then what hope would humans have of ever controlling them? Quite a few smart people are beginning worry about this."

John—"Yes, but bear in mind that up to now computers can only do what they have been programmed to do, and they cannot make mistakes, and best of all they are not egotists like humans. They do what they are told. Abraham Lincoln said there are two kinds of people who never amount to much in life, those who cannot do what they are told, and those who cannot do anything but what they are told. Computers and AI up to now fall into the latter category. They are very useful fast efficient idiots. The issue is whether computers can ever learn to program themselves about something that has not already been programmed into their computer memories. If they are never able to truly program themselves then if humans make sure they never tell them to do anything antisocial then it won't happen. You can also build a case that humans are also incapable of programming themselves to do something that has not already been programmed in their memories."

Ellen—"I majored in accounting in college but I took some computer courses and learned a little something about programming but nothing we studied was remotely like what you are talking about here. It is one thing to figure out how much money a business made in one year or what its assets and liabilities are but to think you could develop a system to produce and distribute goods all around Earth in an optimal fashion is off the charts. I don't think it could ever be done."

Bubba—"I'm with you Ellen. I'm a farmer and I shore don't want nobody tellin' me what to produce and who to sell it to. That's pure socialism or communism. It's un-American that's what it is. Hell, anybody should know that's nothin' but bullshit. Excuse my French."

Hellen—"Being a nurse I can tell you no computer can ever take over my job. Somebody has got to be there face-to-face to help people when they get sick or hurt. You can use all the computers you want to diagnose diseases and prescribe treatments but there is no way you can program a computer to do what nurses do, such as give someone a shot for example, or take blood pressure. Such treatment would be part of the necessities of life, but it could not be allocated or produced by a computer, or would the computer decide who would be given treatment or not, in effect make decisions about who would live or die because of having some sort of disease or accident?"

Judy—"I'm just a housewife too and I can tell you it would be nice for many of us to know that we would be entitled to food, clothing, shelter, and medical treatment because somebody gave us one share of stock in Spaceship Earth, Inc. What would it do? Have our necessities of life delivered to our doorsteps using something like Amazon or Fed Ex? I'm all for it. Bring it on as soon as possible."

Andy—"Police services would be considered a necessity of life. How would a computer allocate what us cops do? Some things just cannot be decided by computers. Or is it this wonderful computer system would somehow get rid of bad guys. Would everyone being born rich so they did not have to work eliminate crime? I doubt it. Some criminals just enjoy being criminals. They do it just for the fun of it. They enjoy trying to make fools out of cops. They get bored just sittin' around doin' nothin'. Seems to me this Spaceship Earth idea would make life boring as dirt."

Adam—"It is interesting that the economics profession has historically had very little to say about the problem of boredom. It was assumed if there were no limited resources that people would have sense enough to figure out how to entertain themselves. Besides this Spaceship Earth idea assumes certain people would want to entertain others. Are you saying Andy that you think some people can only entertain themselves by committing crimes?"

Andy—"No, not necessarily, but I am saying I think some people like to commit crimes to entertain themselves. They get some sort of kick out of it, some sort of psychological charge."

Trudy—"For whatever it's worth I can tell you as a psychotherapist that some people do like to commit crimes to satisfy their psychological needs. There is a psychological Game called Cops and Robbers that has been identified by transactional analysts. People get used to certain kinds of strokes for doing certain kinds of things in early childhood, such as being naughty and trying not to get caught. People play psychological Games of all sorts for stimulus, structure, and recognition. There is more to life than food, clothing, and shelter."

Martin got selected next by The Truther Martin—"It seems to me homelessness is one of the greatest problems in the US and around Spaceship earth, but poverty is the majority cause of homelessness, and mental illness is also a major cause. Many of the homeless are mentally ill, but what caused them to be mentally ill? Poor psychological, social, economic, and political environments. The alternatives include constructing better mental health facilities and more treatment centers, and of course programs to eliminate poverty, such as President Lyndon Johnson's Great Society Program in the nineteen sixties in which he attempted to eliminate poverty in places like Appalachia. It worked for a while, but it did not work for long. Unfortunately he wanted both butter and guns, also pouring more and more money into the disastrous Vietnam War, escalating the long process of contamination of the USian budget and financial system up to now. Poverty in the US is now increasing. Curing poverty entails possibly doing many things, creating more government jobs, infrastructure jobs, entailing raising taxes on the elite rich and large corporations, cutting military expenses among other things. But you can also build the case that the capitalistic system is also to blame. Some stay the solution is more socialism or socialism period. I agree that we need more government ownership and control, more socialism. That's what I recommend. And I recommend Bernie Sanders for president in 2020.

"Thank you, Truther rooster, for finally selecting me to start a new discussion."

Marian—"I am not sure I agree with you that homelessness is the most serious problem right now. I fully agree it is a serious problem for far too many people. As a retired school teacher, I am one of the lucky ones in that I have a defined benefits pension plan, something that is becoming more and more of a rarity in the US. Corporations stopped providing them for most workers many years ago. My husband and I have a better retirement than most people, and we are not particularly worried about homelessness for ourselves. On the other hand, many older retired people are. Most of the homeless I am sure do not have Social Security benefits if they are not old enough to be retired. Almost no one could live independently on the maximum Social Security benefit payment right now. But for sure it helps.

"I recommend that the government increase Social Security benefits by requiring rich people to pay the full Social Security premium on their full incomes, more than only on up to the first two hundred thousand dollars of income per year or whatever it is. That might be enough to keep Social Security solvent for a long time. I have no idea how much it would be feasible to increase Social Security payments but for sure they need to be increased for most people."

Joel—"I agree with you Marian, but the problem is that many people today will never have even the full Social Security benefit however inadequate it might be for retirement income. There are probably millions of people in the US who do not contribute to the Social Security system for a lifetime. There are people working in the so-called underground economy who are paid in cash. They are not listed as employed or unemployed with the government or employers. Many are undocumented migrants. This ties in with the whole employment problem, which is worsened by automation and AI. More and more jobs are being taken over by machines. I read just a few days ago that MacDonald's has now figured out a way to automate its order-taking process. Someone has invented a robot that can take orders and somehow dispense food. So even these low paid labor jobs could be eliminated. Look at all the grocery store check-out clerks that were eliminated by the AI robot check-out machines customers use to check out themselves and pay for their groceries by themselves. Truck drivers they say are at risk of having their jobs eliminated. I can't see how computers driving trucks could ever work, but they say it can. If you eliminate all jobs that require humans to drive some sort of motorized vehicle for a living you are talking about a lot of unemployment.

"The Spaceship Earth article Rout had us read back in Asheville is becoming more and more relevant. I have seen several internet articles advocating basic income schemes. One of the democratic presidential candidates, Yang, advocates allocating one thousand dollars a month to all citizens, which is more than the Social Security benefits of some citizens who retire now. While the one thousand a month would help it would not be enough to live on. The Spaceship Earth plan advocated distributing the necessities of life to all Earthian human citizens which for sure would cure the problem of retirement. In effect no one would ever have to retire under this scheme since the necessity of life shipments would never cease until death, speaking of which, the Spaceship Earth article assumes peaceful natural deaths will result in a significant lowering of Earth's human population through time through natural attrition, natural deaths exceeding births, until Earth's human population reaches a sustainable level.

"The overall problem however is horrendous. What it boils down to is that billions of would-be workers alive around Spaceship Earth are basically unneeded as workers. You don't need that many manual labor workers anymore as a percentage of the human population. What you need are thinkers and problem solvers, mind workers, if you will. Buckminster Fuller said in his book *Operating Manual for Spaceship Earth* governments could eliminate all unemployment overnight by awarding mind grants to all citizens. You don't need that many billionaires, people who don't work at all but who travel around and do whatever they want to consuming many times more resources than poor people that do manual work thanks to the wealth they have inherited and/or amassed. And you don't need billionaires to provide surplus money for investments, grants, and such. Central bankers of sovereign governments can create all the new funny money they need for this by just punching digits into computers and calling the numbers money.

"The reality is that to produce and allocate resources and goods in the long run using the economic policies and systems we use now without significant peaceful population decreases using natural attrition the small percentage of humans employed in thinking and problem-solving jobs would have to sit back and watch billions of humans go extinct, in an extinction process somewhat analogous to what happened to the millions of native inhabitants living for over a thousand years in what is now called North, Central, and

South America, after European Earthians discovered their so-called "New World" in 1497.

"On the other hand, it seems to me there is little chance Yang's idea of one thousand dollars per month of basic permanent income happening in the US. And imagine trying to implement something like this around Spaceship Earth, now populated by almost eight billion humans, mostly in poor countries.

"I recommend however at least trying to implement something like Spaceship Earth as soon as possible, which would require a serious overhaul of the capitalistic system. Just saying we need socialism is tantamount to saying nothing because there is nothing concrete in such a statement, just poppycock and blather.

"The best way to get rich around Spaceship Earth from here on is to reduce the Earthian human population through peaceful natural attrition in a humane way to provide larger and larger pieces of annual economic pie cut for individuals from smaller and smaller economic pies baked every year, requiring less and less destruction of Earthian resources, fossil fuel consumption, and global warming."

The Truther rooster crowed while selecting Sam.

Sam—"Well, it seems to me right now that the biggest economic and political problem around Spaceship Earth is this matter of polarization. Not only in the United States but around the world people are getting more set in their ways and are getting angrier as their economic and political plights worsen, as their incomes stagnate or go down, as their lives become more and more precarious. Here we are on the cusp of another global recession or depression, probably worse than 2007. Trump is in the White House and Biden is being touted as the frontrunner of the DNC. Biden's the obvious choice of the corrupt DNC and the Deep State as the Democratic presidential candidate for 2020 to run against Trump. We will again be faced with the choice of choosing the lesser of two evils, picked and manipulated by two corrupt political parties to serve the interest of establishment politicians and the deep state, not citizens of the US, much less citizens of Spaceship Earth.

"Perhaps most worrisome is what seems to be an increasing anger and tendency to violence among and between extremists on the left and right. I read on the internet that regardless of who wins in 2020 there could be violence and bloodshed. We have scattered shootings now by extremists or terrorists or whatever you want to call them in the US. This sort of thing could worsen after the presidential election of 2020.

"Regarding the alternatives for dealing with this I suppose the best thing we can do is resort back once again to the hope for a better day strategy. Since there are no known answers at present. What could be done that has not been tried? This Game-free seminar approach was supposed to help correct this problem. Well, we have been talking in this group for several months now and I can't tell it has done one whit worth of good in the broader environment. We have learned to tolerate one another more in this group given our diverse backgrounds, but what about similar groups in the outside world in the meantime. They have not gotten more OK. We have got nothing but politics as usual and more kicking the can down the road. People are more polarized now than ever. Humans not only in the US but in most European countries are following a similar path, and right-wing extremists are probably gaining the upper hand. It looks like humans are inexorably heading into a dystopian fascistic world with less freedom, less human dignity, less human security, with global warming and climate change hanging over their heads, like a Sword of Damocles.

"I recommend that Rout and his donors make public what has happened in this group and spread the word that people can learn to get along better and see the viewpoints of other polarized people better if subjected to a Game-free group process such as this, especially if you pay them five thousand dollars a month to do it. The problem is where are you going to get the kind of money these rich donors have coughed up for this experimental group. Sure, you can bribe people to get together in groups such as this if you have enough money, but how could this ever happen generally in the real world. Most rich people like being rich and they are not going to willingly give up their riches and power, which they think they deserve and honestly won.

"But that's about all I can think of recommending right now. For sure I do not recommend any sort of military action. That has been disastrous in the last five or six decades. Socialism? Big deal. How is it possible to even dream of making something like this happen anytime soon? And what is socialism? There is no clear-cut definition of socialism, what degree of socialism etc. We already have much socialism in the US, and have had for decades. More taxes? Sure, raise the taxes of the rich as much as you can, but good luck, since rich taxpayers have already bought off the politicians, and voters keep voting for their friends who will also be bought off in Washington, inundated as it is with billions of dollars of bribery money flowing around the place like flood water from a massive hurricane. Infrastructure spending? Yes, for sure. But where is the money going to come from? Yes, seriously raise taxes on the rich sending tax rates back to eighty percent or more, back to where it was before Ronald Reagan started a long Republican tax-cut war by the elite rich and large corporations, but good luck making it happen. Do you want to keep creating more funny money? Money is almost worthless now. Seventeen percent of all sovereign debt around Spaceship Earth is now negative interest rate money. People are loaning their worthless money to their governments at negative interest rates just hoping they will get some of it back in ten or more years. How fucked up can an economic system get?

"So, I recommend to you my fellow Spaceship Earth De-Gaming group members that you keep taking five thousand dollars for one day's work bullshitting as long as the donors see fit to dole it out. And I recommend trying to set up similar groups around Spaceship Earth as soon as possible by any means possible. The only hope is to create new peaceful consensual answers to create new economic and political policies and systems that work for all humans. What Earthians have now is not working. No kind of economic system has ever worked for everyone. Let us all at least grieve together. It's better than shooting one another."

Joel—"I agree with you Sam. Somehow humans must improve their communication systems. One can build a case right now the Earthian human world is insane. Most economic and political systems are obsolete and dysfunctional for eighty or so percent of humans alive on Earth, but some are satisfied, the rich and powerful, and the brainwashed poor who think believing what they are told is satisfying, since this makes them superior to non-believers, believing believing what they believe will cause them to live in eternal bliss after they die.

"The only hope somehow is for Earthian humans to construct better educational systems. And I am not talking about the current school and university educational systems around Earth. I am talking about the total educational process, starting at birth, the whole set of messages humans are exposed to from biological parents and others in their earliest years, and even the electro-chemical messages they receive in the wombs of birth mothers. Somehow Earthian humans must be given permission to think about reality itself, from an early age, not just believe what they are told, in many cases by parents who do not have a clue about what is really going on themselves, and may not care what is really going on, who spend most of their free time watching soap operas, sports and entertainments and distractions of all sorts, including political, religious, and Hollywood fantasy."

Luke—"Ah, the one and only Joel, the fount of wisdom has spoken. And after several months of brain-washing I must say I am beginning to agree with him. I must admit I don't believe like I did, and I mightily fear in my heart of hearts that this might get me sent to hell for losing my faith. I still believe the one true Lord God is merciful. Maybe He will understand how this group made me do it, knowing how much I needed the money. Maybe he will forgive me since it was not my fault."

Albert—"Don't worry Luke. I think you will be fine. One thing no one has brought up in our discussions is that in the beginning there was nothing in the universe except bosons and quarks. There were no Earthian humans. Everything evolved from that sort of state over eons. Humans came along several billion years after the first bosons and quarks started evolving into higher matter. If we go back to that so what. It will be part of a natural process, global warming or no global warming, another event in cosmic history. As to there being an alternative universe or universes nobody has ever seen before, even with the most powerful telescopes, it seems to me there might be, but it's basically unprovable, just like the notion of life after death."

Sam—"Regarding the argument there must be something there or millions of people would not believe like Luke used to believe, it seems to me all religions came about because of the inherent unfairness, precarity, and banality of human life. People knew they would inevitably die, which was sad enough, and they knew that pain and misery could befall them at any time. Were they happy? Sure, for fleeting moments but most of the time they lived under dread and anxiety, that caused them to fight for more resources than they really needed, trying to steal for gain and power and wealth, and so forth, and it caused them to assume there must be some sort of god-like forces making things happen, so they developed various religious systems, wasting a lot of resources trying to bribe their gods into being nice to them personally instead of their enemies. In my opinion those who imagined there were multiple gods making things happen were more realistic than those who imagined there was only one god making everything happen, since this is more analogous to the real human emotions and satisfactions they experienced, given that any reasonably bright human should have known that natural events were causing the plights of various members of their families and communities. Some died of this that or the other, some were killed by wild animals, snakes, and so forth, some were killed by hostile tribes. Some seemed to get through their short brutish lives much easier and better than others. Yet many Earthian humans assumed some sort of god must have blessed the most fortunate, while they assumed those who had horrible difficulties and problems probably deserved punishment by a god for not doing what he or she told them to do.

"These effects observed by humans were the results of inevitable infinitely-regressive cause-effect chains inexorably progressing into the future. Most likely there is no free will; if so, everything is either accidental or inevitable, depending on how you look at it. Events are like dominoes falling in infinite cause-effect chains. Every event is both an effect and a cause of other events. Rather than see that some people were merely unlucky enough to be the results of cause-effect chains producing certain diseases and negative events and others were lucky enough to be the result of cause-effect chains inevitably producing good health, good looks, intelligence, wealth, prestige, power, etc., they assumed gods and humans were making these anomalous unfair events happen, and thus various individuals deserved to be reviled, pitied, admired, praised, rewarded, condemned, punished, exterminated, etc. This unmanaged unfair process enabled various kinds of power people (priests, preachers, kings, queens, barons, presidents, fascist dictators, corporate CEOs, generals, etc.) with communication skill and charisma to dominate weaker humans who believed power people were chosen favorites of the god(s), and thus were entitled to require weaker humans to hand over to them as their god-ordained rulers labor, food, money, and other necessities of life, for performing rituals and playing psychological Games, i.e. for Persecuting, Rescuing, and Victimizing various kinds of humans, groups, and organizations, practicing mumbo-jumbo.

"The best hope for Earthian life is that new group imagoes, scripts, schemata, and behaviors will be caused to be evolved in human brains, hopefully causing humans around Earth to implement Game-free democratic I'm OK—You're OK groups such as this one, that will help change a disastrous mindless master-servant I'm OK—You're Not OK authoritarian course that about fifty percent or so of humans around Spaceship Earth have set, heading full-sail into hell on Earth."

The Covid Response

After it became obvious the Covid-19 pandemic was real, Rout Logger decided to discontinue his Spaceship Earth group in its present format after considering and discussing several options with the group donors. He notified the group members in this email message:

July 1, 2020

Dear Spaceship Earth Group members,

After giving the matter considerable thought consulting with the group donors, I have decided the best option at this time is to discontinue the discussions of our group because of the Covid-19 pandemic.

I appreciate very much your participation and the contributions each of you made to our group meetings. In my opinion, and in the opinion of the group donors, the project was a success, achieving several of the goals set at the beginning, a major one being to demonstrate how Earthian humans from disparate walks of life can learn how not to play psychological Games in discussion groups, while co-constructing better time structuring patterns, transactional patterns, life positions, and scripts for dealing with existential problems.

Another five-thousand-dollar bank deposit has been made to the Spaceship Earth bank account set up for each of you as a form of severance pay. I intended to conduct the group for a year or more, but the Covid-19 virus made that infeasible using a face-to-face format.

The donors and I seriously considered establishing some sort of zoom-like process wherein our group would continue to meet in virtual reality using computers and the internet, after furnishing each of you a home computer with a large screen to use for group meetings, but we ultimately decided not to do it.

The donors and I however have decided to fund the development a new computer program for audio-visual internet virtual reality group discussion. We have formed a new non-profit corporation, a real Spaceship Earth, Inc., designed to research, develop, and produce new computer code and programming for such a system. We have hired several high-tech experts who are now working on the new system.

The Spaceship Earth, Inc. virtual reality computer system will be able to accommodate up to forty group members who can be shown around the perimeters of computer screens. A digital Truther rooster, replete with rooster-crowing capability, positioned in the center of the screen, will be digitally spun to randomly-select a Leader of the Moment in a process analogous to the process we used manually in our face-to-face group sessions. After the spinning and rooster crowing ceases the Truther-selected leader will be enlarged on the screen as he or she does and says what we have been doing and saying face-to-face in response to The Truther selection process in hotel room meetings: Define the problem(s), Delineate the alternative(s), and Make recommendations.

We will have a procedure programmed into the system that will enable participants to digitally raise their hands, after the The Truther-selected leader decides to stop talking, to respond to what the The Truther-selected leader said. The first hand to go up will speak next, and other respondents will speak in the order in which they raised their hands, using the same procedure we used in our hotel meetings regarding time allowed for speaking. We will program-in a hand-raising process here, which I did not allow face to face, because of the technical difficulties required to make sure Game- players cannot corrupt Game-free Adult democratic rules in digital time. As usual, no speaker will be interrupted before s/he decides to stop speaking, provided the group moderator does not decide a speaker is deliberately killing time conducting a filibuster sabotage, such as used in the USian senate, maliciously attempting to destroy democratic discussion. Group members attempting to destroy democracy will be summarily muted and banished from the screen.

We hope to have the system up and running in a year or so, at which time we will use the system with Spaceship Earth chapters we will establish around Earth that will download the new democratic computerized system for their groups who will use the same Game-free process we used in hotel rooms, to facilitate Adult discussions of existential psychological, social, economic, religious, and political states of affairs, primarily to help stave off Earthian extinction caused by human-caused global warming, climate change, and nuclear war, caused by obsolete and dangerous Earthian human feeling, thinking, understanding, believing, and doing.

Thanks again for your help and contributions toward making this project a success.

Best wishes to you all,

Rout Logger

5

HOW IT WOUND UP

Group members were not surprised Rout decided to cancel The Group meetings because of the Covid pandemic. They had no desire to go to monthly meetings requiring air travel exposing them to the Corona virus in airports, airplanes, hotels, and restaurants; but most were surprised that Rout decided to discontinue The Group permanently. They thought he would start it back up after the Corona problem went away. They were also surprised he gave them another five thousand dollars in severance pay July 1, 2020. They had not been paid for cancelled meetings in the months of April, May, and June of 2020.

Rout and the donors seriously considered using some sort of zoom process with the members working from home in group meetings, but they decided this was not feasible using available technology.

The group members were disappointed things turned out as they did and felt a sense of loss. While some criticized and resented Rout's rules, arbitrary decisions, blunt talk, and stern uncaring demeanor at the beginning they had found the overall experience to be satisfying, and they knew they had been well compensated for their time and participation.

Rout was surprised at how quickly his group members adapted to increase their social OKness, proving in his mind and in the minds of a majority of his donor group that the random-selection Adult— Adult Game-free I'm OK—You're OK democratic process, motivated by a spinning crowing three-foot-tall copper rooster Truther, used to randomly select leaders of the moment to start discussions, increased OKness among his group members, and would produce similar results around Earth were it widely used with similar groups.

He and the group donors decided this six-month experiment was good enough to call The Rooster Truther Group experiment a success, so they decided to disband the group to focus instead on developing software for a new computer-based democratic Adult—Adult I'm OK—You're OK Game- free system, in a new non-profit corporation called Spaceship Earth, Inc., to change dysfunctional social level transactions around Spaceship Earth as soon and widely as possible, to encourage and foster liberty, equality, and fraternity, and to diminish Earthian existential threats.

Rout had used random-selection devices coordinating case method discussions with his students in schools and trainees in organizations and groups, and he knew the process had worked with them; but he had not used a discussion De-Gamer with a group as heterogeneous as this group, containing participants from different walks of life and persuasions representing different age groups, sexual orientations, religions, races, educational levels, vocations and professions, socioeconomic levels, and political parties. He was relieved that things worked out as well as they did.

Humans have an instinctual liking for games that have fair rules. When a kid cheats, other kids loudly and quickly call out the cheater and complain about the behavior. Children especially seem to like random-selection processes, a favorite childhood game being "Spin the Bottle". Games of chance such as monopoly are popular. Spinners such as the Truther Rooster used in learning situations cathects Fair Child Ego States in the participants that rubberband, or bring to the present, pleasant feelings of childhood that have a positive effect on the OKness and transactional patterns of older participants in the here and now. All children are born psychologically and socially OK and stay that way until they are contaminated and corrupted by humans around them who have been contaminated and corrupted by Not-OK ego states, transactions, script massages, Games, time structuring patterns, and rackets, partially caused by Not-OK economic and political systems, religions, and cultures.

In effect the new computer-based Adult—Adult I'm OK—You're OK Game-free discussion system is designed to create a new type of tv and internet social game, a fair De-Gaming game in which all players win. Hopefully the new computer-based Adult—Adult I'm OK—You're OK Game-free discussion system and fraternal democracy chapters will take root and evolve in usage around Spaceship Earth to produce results analogous to those produced by The Rooster Truther Group, eventually evolving free and fair group participation by many millions of Earthian humans. What is the probability this will happen? Probably less than .25, but Rout and most of his donors thought the goal was worth pursuing. All the donors have a lot of money and they were glad to wager some of it on something that might produce truly significant social results for all Earthian humans. Some of the donors had already tried to no avail to get the I'm OK—You're Not OK USian government to increase their income taxes to provide money for infrastructure projects to help lower-class and middle-class USian citizens; but this was prevented by I'm OK— You're Not OK USian presidents and congress people who were financed and bribed by I'm OK—You're Not OK elite rich citizens and large corporations (primarily repugnant Repugs but also dim Dems) who did not want their income taxes increased.

One donor thought the new proposed computer-based Adult—Adult Game-free I'm OK—You're OK democratic sortition discussion system might become the social equivalent of a Salk vaccine to prevent violence around Spaceship Earth. Without doubt the USian government is in need of such a process in all its branches, as are all Earthian governments; but the process is especially needed by the haughty high and mighty I'm OK—You're Not OK USian government dealing with other nations under leaders similar to Trump, playing over and over since 1945 second and third-degree versions of the one-up psychological Game NIGYSOB, Now I've Got You, You SOB, using Not OK covert psychological sabotages, overt sanctions, military shooting on the ground, and bombing.

Systems somewhat similar to Rout Logger's proposed Spaceship Earth computer-based Adult—Adult Game-free I'm OK—You're OK democratic group discussion system presented in this novel are now up and running on tv news networks. The new zoom technology is gaining more and more acceptance, affecting tv shows and newscasts, and is widely used by various private individuals, groups, and organizations. Some tv networks are already using processes similar to what Rout conceived with three or four experts shown on tv screens at once who are zoomed into focus when it's their time to talk about what's in the news, in the opinion of show hosts and bosses of tv networks. The new proposed Spaceship Earth, Inc. computer-based Adult-Adult Game-Free I'm OK—You're OK democratic system will be able to assimilate and accommodate up to forty group participants and a group leader positioned around the perimeter of one computer screen, with a virtual reality The Truther rooster pictured in the center of the screen, a rooster that raucously crows when spun to randomly-select Leaders of the Moment by pointing them out, that could be live streamed by groups and organizations around Spaceship Earth into billions of computer screens connected to the internet.

TV networks have not yet set up a fully democratic Game-free I'm OK—You're OK Adult—Adult Spaceship Earth-type program with participants randomly-selected from disparate walks of real life who are randomly-selected as Leaders of the Moment in group sessions to start a democratic discussion of a relevant Earthian problem, by defining and discussing a serious problem of the moment in her or his opinion happening anywhere around Spaceship Earth, that includes delineating alternatives for dealing with the problem and making recommendations for something to do about the problem, that is then democratically discussed dialectically by group members with fully equal rights and responsibilities in the discussion group. Most current tv newscasts use more Parent and Child ego state transactions than any other kind. Fully Adult ego state transactions rarely occur. Most newscasters and their guest commentators are primarily concerned about pleasing their bosses and audiences playing relatively innocuous low-degree variants of psychological Games such as GEE, YOU'RE WONDERFUL, Ms. or Mr. NEWSCASTER, AIN'T IT AWFUL, and GREENHOUSE using Adapted Child and Critical Parent ego states. While most of the content is true or not fake it rarely enables audiences to comprehend what is really going on in complex psychological and social states of affairs.

After the The Truther rooster randomly-selected Leader of the Moment decides to stop talking in the new zoom-like tv and internet system, other group members will discuss the problem the leader brought up honestly and truthfully agreeing or disagreeing with what the leader said in the order in which they raise their hands until the discussion runs out of steam, at which time The Truther will be spun again if time remains in the session.

I'm OK—You're Not OK group members who play filibuster-like psychological Games talking just for sake of talking or to sabotage the development of co-constructed consensual democratic answers playing psychological Games will be summarily brought to a halt by a loud clanging cowbell. Unrepentant miscreant members of the group will be permanently banished from the screen.

Rout's experimental group entailed conducting discussion sessions three hours long without a break. Most likely sessions broadcasted and live streamed to large tv and internet audiences would need to be limited to about one hour to maximize learning effectiveness.

How to reward participants is an issue. Will Earthian humans participate for strokes, belonging, structure, stimulation, recognition, personal achievement, and personal satisfaction? Can Earthian humans learn to look upon themselves as equal I'm OK—You're OK stockholders of Spaceship Earth, Inc., co-constructing with fellow stockholders around Spaceship Earth democratic consensual answers for managing Spaceship Earth states of affairs from the bottom up?

Would Spaceship Earth fraternal democracy chapter discussions be entertaining enough to be shown on tv and internet networks?

Would members of the elite rich in the upper hierarchies of large organizations such as Harrison in Rout's Group learn to accept or tolerate the computer-based system and the salutary benefits of the random selection I'm OK—You're OK Adult—Adult Game-free discussion process, considering almost all transactions in large organizations up and down a chain of command are I'm OK—You're Not OK, I'm Not OK—Your're OK Parent—Child and Child—Parent transactions?

They might accept the system if they thought it might eventually lead to all Earthian humans receiving Spaceship Earth, Inc. dividend checks similar to those proposed in the essay, "The Evolution of Spaceship Earth, Inc.", at https://blog. effectivelearning.net/the-evolution-of-spaceship- earth-inc-3/.

Not all members of Rout's discussion group or the donor group agreed that this group experiment had been a success. A sizeable minority of both group members and donors were convinced The Group could not have been formed had the participants not been bribed with money to participate and the seeming OKness increases produced in the group was pseudo OKness that was produced not by genuine structural changes within the psyches of the participants but by Rout's dictatorial rules and demeanor and his threats to banish participants if they refused to abide by the group's I'm OK—You're OK Adult ego state Game-free democratic rules and laws.

According to this view, fundamental laws of cause-effect human nature cannot be changed and as soon as the money and the group meetings stop the participants of this group will revert to their previous levels of OKness or Not OKness. This view assumes humans are inherently mercenary and self-interested and will only do what they perceive will enhance their personal life positions, only doing what they think will do them some good. Such a view proposes humans from the moment of birth are incessantly goaded, cajoled, intimidated, and threatened into doing what they do by various and sundry differentiated inexorably and ineluctably-progressing infinitely-regressive cause-effect chains in families and in various and sundry groups and organizations generating differentiated psychological and social script messages, group imagoes, scripts, rewards, and punishments that through time create internal psychological feeling, thinking, knowing, believing, and doing structures and programs in individual Earthian human brains and nervous systems that never change, barring *force majeure* events.

Rout and a small majority of his group members and donors agree with the proposition that individual Earthian humans are closed systems that cannot change using free will their subconscious feeling, thinking, and behaving structures that have been introjected into, embedded, and ingrained in their brain cells and nervous systems through time; but they also believe—if external states of nature can be changed to some degree by current Adult— Adult I'm OK—You're OK

Game-free democratic co-constructed consensual answers—co-constructed by large numbers of Earthian humans from all walks of life correcting Not OK predetermined OKness life positions, time structuring patterns, ego states, transactional patterns, Games, Rackets, script messages, and life scripts—Spaceship Earth can be saved. They think there is some chance the new Spaceship Earth Adult—Adult I'm OK—You're OK Game-free democratic computer-based discussion system widely downloaded into computers around Spaceship Earth by I'm OK—You're OK fraternal democracy chapters might cause I'm OK—You're Not OK authoritarian psychological, social, economic, religious, educational, governmental, military, and political organizations to change in such a way as to eliminate the probability of human extinction.

Some of the observable social OKness increases in The Group were no doubt caused by nothing more mysterious than the participants being forced to communicate in Game-free I'm OK—You're OK Adult—Adult democratic ways with humans from disparate walks of life. This in effect changed the state of nature of the participants. Having lunch with and shooting the bull with disparate unequal group participants before and after formal group sessions caused many of them to feel more OK about themselves and others. Whether they will revert to their previous levels of OKness or Not-OKness now that the group has been disbanded making them dependent on their naturally-evolved inherited cause-effect chains of family members, friends, groups, and organizations for strokes, stimulation, recognition, belonging, and money remains to be seen.

And that's OK, if free will does not exist and all Earthian humans are caused to be how they are. If that is the case, then no one, even Trump, is to blame or praise for how they are. Martin Buber said in his book *I and Thou* that humans are simultaneously responsible and non-responsible for how they are. Ludwig Wittgenstein said in his book *Prototractatus* that everything that happens happens by accident. It's also possible that everything that happens is simultaneously accidental and inevitable, another antinomy. Another proposition formulated by Wittgenstein is that "The case is all there is."

Rich I'm OK—You're OK donors in their golden years bored with watching their investment accounts automatically increase by thousands and millions of dollars every year, a billion or more in some years, can donate billions of their surplus currency units to Spaceship Earth, Inc. to hire computer experts to flow chart and write code for the new Spaceship Earth computer-based Game-free I'm OK—You're OK Adult—Adult ego state system, and to purchase thousands of laptop computers for group members; pay internet service provider fees; recruit, establish, and administer Spaceship Earth I'm OK—You're OK Game-free Adult—Adult fraternal democracy chapters; and download the new program into billions of Earthian laptop computers, tablets, and mobile devices, to help prevent not only the extinction of Earthian *homo sapiens* but also the extinctions of millions of other species of fauna and flora living aboard Spaceship Earth.

6

REFERENCES

Abelson, R.P. (1981). Psychological status of the script concept. *American psychologist*. Vol. 36, No. 7, pp. 715-729.

Abercrombie, M.L.J. (1960). *The anatomy of judgment: An investigation into the processes of perception and reasoning.* Basic Books: New York.

Allen, J.R. and Allen, B.A. (1988). Scripts and permissions: Some unexamined assumptions and connotations. *Transactional analysis journal*, 18, 283-293.

Allen, J.R. and Allen, B.A. (1991). Towards a constructivist TA. In B.R. Loria (Ed.), *The stamford papers: Selections from the 29th annual ITAA conference*, pp. 1-22. Madison, WI: Omnipress.

Allen, J.R. (2003). Concepts, competencies, and interpretative communities. *Transactional analysis journal*, 33(2),126-147.

Allen, J.R. and Allen, B.A. (2005). *Therapeutic journey: Life and practice.* Oakland, CA: Transactional Analysis Press.

Anderson, R.C. (1977). The notion of schemata and the educational enterprise: General discussion of the conference, in *Schooling and the acquisition of knowledge*, Anderson, R.C., Spiro, W.E., and Montague, W.E., (eds.). Hillsdale, N.J.: Lawrence Erlbaum Associates, Publishers.

Baier, Kurt (1958). *The moral point of view: A rational basis of ethics.* Ithaca, N.Y.: Cornell University Press.

Barnes, G., ed. (1977). *Transactional analysis after Eric Berne: Teachings and practices of three TA schools.* New York: Harper's College Press.

Barnes, G. (1994). *Justice, love, and wisdom: Linking psychotherapy to second-order cybernetics.* Zabreb, Croatia: Medicinska Naklada.

Bateson, Gregory. (1972*). Steps to an ecology of mind: The new information sciences can lead to a new understanding of man.* New York: Ballantine Books. 729

Bedeian, A (2002). The dean's disease: How the darker side of power manifests itself in the office of the dean. *Academy of Management Learning and Education,* 1 (2), 164-173.

Belmont, J.M. (1989). Cognitive strategies and strategic learning. *American psychologist,* Vol. 44, No. 2, pp. 142-148.

Bennett, J.B. (1971). *Good writing.* Boston, MA: Intercollegiate Case Clearing House, Harvard College.

Berne, Eric (1957). Ego states in psychotherapy. *American Journal of Psychotherapy,* 11:2.

Berne, Eric (1957). *A layman's guide to psychiatry and psychoanalysis.* New York: Simon and Schuster.

Berne, Eric (1963). *The structure and dynamics of organizations and groups.* New York: Grove Press.

Berne, E. (1964). *Games people play: The psychology of human relationships.* New York: Grove Press.

Berne, E. (1966). *Principles of group treatment.* New York: Grove Press.

Berne, Eric. (1970) *What do you say after you say hello? The psychology of human destiny.* New York: Grove Press.

Bierman, H.; Bonini, C.; and Hauseman, W. (1969). *Quantitative analysis for business decisions.* Homewood, Ill.: Richard D. Irwin, Inc.

Bird, B.J. (1989). *Entrepreneurial behavior.* Glenview, IL: Scot, Foresman and Company.

Bienvenu, B. (1969). *New priorities in training: A guide for industry.* New York: American Management Association.

Brandt, S.C. (1989). Foreword. *New business ventures and the entrepreneur.* Stevenson, H.H., Roberts, M.J., and Grousbeck, H.I. Homewood, Ill: Irwin.

Buber, M. (1958). *I and Thou.* Translated by Ronald Gregor Smith. New York: Charles Scribner's Sons.

Buber, M. (1966). *The way of response.* N.N. Glatzer, (ed.), New York: Schocken Books.

Buber, M. (1969). Genuine dialogue and the possibilities of peace (M. Friedman, trans.). In E.W. Williams & H. Zahn (Eds.), *Men of dialogue: Martin Buber and Albrecht Goes* (pp. 20-27), New York: Funk & Wagnalls. (Original work published 1957).

Carland, J.C., Carland, J.W. and Stewart, W. (1996). Seeing what's not there: The enigma of entrepreneurship. *Proceedings of the 20th National Small Business Consulting Conference*, San Diego, CA., pp. 3-8.

Carlson, R. (1981). Studies in script theory: Adult analogs of a childhood nuclear scene. *Journal of personality and social psychology*, Vol. 40, No. 3, pp. 501-510.

Carter, J. (2006). *Palestine: Peace not apartheid.* New York: Simon & Schuster.

Cates, J.N. and Sussman, M.B. (1992). Family systems and inheritance. *Family business review,* Vol. V, No. 2, pp. 205-226

Chacko, T.I. (1983). Student ratings of instruction: A function of grading standards. Educational Research Quarterly, 8 (2), 20-25.

Childs-Gowell, E. (1979). *Bodyscript Blockbusting.* Seattle, Washington.

Childs-Gowell, E. (1992). *Good Grief Rituals.* Station Hill Press. Childs-Gowell, E. (2001). *Regression and protection: How to provide safety when working with deeply wounded clients.* Seattle, Washington.

Christensen, C.R. and Hanson, A.J. (1986*). Teaching and the case method.* New York: Mc-Graw-Hill.

Christensen, C.R., Garvin, D.A., & Sweet, A. (Eds.). (1991). *Education for judgment: The artistry of discussion leadership.* Boston: Harvard Business School Press.

Christensen, C.R. (1992*). Education for judgment: The artistry of discussion leadership.* New York: Mc-Graw-Hill.

Chomsky, N. (1987). *The chomsky reader,* J. Peck, ed. New York: Pantheon books.

Chomsky, N. (2005). *Imperial ambitions: Conversations on the post-9/11 world, interviews with David Barsamian.* New York: Henry Holt and Company.

Clarke, J.I. and Dawson, C. (1998). *Growing up again: Parenting ourselves, parenting our children.* Center City: Minn.: Hazelden, 1998. Clarke, J.L. (1999). *Connections: The threads that strengthen families.* Center City, Minnesota: Hazelden.

Cockburn, A. (2007, May 14). Is global warming a sin? *The Nation*, Vol 284, No. 19.

Cohen, A.R, Fink, S, Gadon, H. & Willits, R. (1992). *Effective behavior in organizations: Learning from the interplay of cases, concepts, and student experiences* (5th ed.). Homewood, Ill: Irwin.

Cohn, M. (1990). *Passing the torch: Transfer strategies for your family business.* US: Liberty Hall Press.

Collins, O. and Moore, D. (1970). *The organization makers: A behavioral study of independent entrepreneurs.* New York: Appleton-Crofts.

Collins, J.C. & Lazier, W.C. (1995). *Managing the small to mid-sized company.* Chicago: Richard D. Irwin, Inc.

Cooper, M. (2007, Sept. 10/17). GOP clutches at Iowa straws: The party's burdened by an unpopular war. *The Nation,* Vol. 285, No. 7.

Cornell, W.F. (1988). Life script theory: A critical review from a developmental perspective. *Transactional Analysis Journal,* 18, 270-282.

Cox, William John. (2004). *You're not stupid! Get the truth: A brief on the Bush Presidency.* Joshua Tree, CA: Progressive Press.

Darwin, C. (1859). *The origin of species: By means of natural selection or The preservation of favored races in the struggle for life.* Reprinted 1998. New York: The Modern Library.

Dawkins, R. (2004). *The ancestor's tale: A pilgrimage to the dawn of evolution.* New York: Houghton Mifflin Company.

Dennis, W. J. (1993*). A small business primer.* Washington, D.C.: National Federation of Independent Business.

Dennis, W.J. (2000*). NFIB Small Business Policy Guide.* Washington, D.C.: National Federation of Independent Business.

Dewey, John. (1935). *Democracy in education: An introduction to the philosophy of education.* New York: The Macmillan Company.

de Young, J. (1991). *Cases in small business management: A strategic problems approach.* Dover, New Hampshire: Upstart Publishing Company, Inc.

Doherty, W.J. (1997). *The intentional family: How to build family ties in our modern world.* Reading, Mass.: Addison-Wesley.

Dooley, A.R., & Skinner, W. (1977, April). Casing case method methods. *Academy of Management Review,* 2(2).

Drego, Pearl (2005). Acceptance speech on receiving the 2004 Eric Berne Memorial Award at Edinburgh, Scotland. *Transactional analysis journal.* Vol. 33, No. 1, pp. 7-30.

Diamond, J. (2006). Collapse: *How societies choose to fail or succeed.* New York: Viking Penguin.

Dressel.(1961*).Evaluation in higher education.* Boston: Houghton Mifflin Company.

Dusay, J. (1972). Egograms and the constancy hypothesis. *Transactional Analysis Journal.* 2(3), 37-41.

Eagle Executive (2006). University impacts region by more than $650 million. Jim Davis, editor, Vol. 20,

No. 1, pg. 12. Statesboro, GA: College of Business Administration, Georgia Southern University.

Eckblad, G. (1981). *Scheme theory: A conceptual framework for cognitive-motivational processes.* London: Academic Press.

Egan, T. (2006). *The worst hard time: The untold story of those who survived the great American dust bowl.* New York: Houghton Mifflin.

English, F. (1971). The substitution factor: Rackets and real feelings, Part I," *Transactional Analysis Journal.* 1(4), 27-32.

English, F. (1972). Rackets and real feelings, Part II. *Transactional Analysis Journal.* 2(1), 23-25.

English, F. (1988). Whither scripts? *Transactional Analysis Journal,* 18, 292-303.

Ernst, F. (1971). The OK corral: The grid for get on with. *Transactional Analysis Journal,* 1971, 1(4), 231-240

Ernst, K (1972). *Games students play, and what to do about them.* Millbrae, CA: Celestial Arts Publishing,

Erskine, R. and Moursund, J. (1988). *Integrative psychotherapy in action.* Highland, New York: The Gestalt Journal Press, Inc.

Fischer, Judith, D. (2004). The use and effects of student ratings in legal writing courses: A plea for holistic evaluation of teaching. *Legal writing: The journal of the legal writing institute,* Volume 10.

Fontaine, James (1838). *A Tale of the Huguenots or Memoirs of a French Refugee Family*, Translated and Compiled from the Original Manuscripts of James Fontaine by One of His Descendants, with an Introduction by F.J. Hawkes, D.D.,stithvalley.com/ fontaine/ memoirsj.htm. The manuscript was first published by John S. Taylor, Theological and Sunday School Bookseller, Corner of Park Row and Spruce Street, New York, 1838.

Forbes (2003). B-Schools: The payback. *Forbes magazine*, October 13, 2003, 172(8), 72-74.

Freire, Paulo (1970). *Pedagogy of the oppressed.* New York: Herder and Herder.

Freud, S. (1933). *The complete introductory lectures on psychoanalysis.* James Strachey (Trans. and Ed.), 1965. New York: W.W. Norton & Company, Inc., 1966.

Fuller, R.B. (1969). *Operating manual for spaceship earth.* New York: Simon and Schuster.

Gagne, R.M. (1977). *The conditions of learning* (3rd. ed.). Holt, Rinehart & Winston.

Gellert, S.A. (1983*). Nuts come in pairs: All you ever wanted to know about couples' relationships and were afraid to ask.* New York: Cite Press.

Gilligan, James (1997). *Violence: Reflections on a national epidemic.* New York: Random House.

Ginsberg, Eli (1966). *The development of human resources.* New York: McGraw-Hill Book Company.

Gioia, D.A. and Poole, P.P. (1984). Scripts in organizational behavior. *Academy of Management Review,* Vol. 9, No. 3, pp. 449-459.

Giroux, Henry. (1992). *Border crossings: Cultural workers and the politics of education.* New York: Routledge.

Goldman, A.L. (1970). *A theory of human action.* New Jersey: Princeton University Press.

Gore, A. (2007). *The assault on reason.* New York: The Penguin Press.

Goulding, R. and Goulding, M. (1976). Injunctions, decisions, and redecisions. *Transactional Analysis Journal,* 6(1), 41-48.

Gragg, C.I. (1940). Because wisdom can't be told. Originally published in the *Harvard Magazine*. In R. Stapleton (ed.), *The Entrepreneur: Concepts and Cases on Creativity in Business*. Lanham, Maryland: University Press of America, 1985.

Graham, Benjamin (1973). *The Intelligent Investor*. New copyrighted material added by Jason Zweig, 2003. New York: HarperCollins Publishers.

Greenwald, A. G., & Gillmore, G. M. (1997a). Grading leniency is a removable contaminant of student ratings. *American Psychologist*, 52 (11), 1209-1216.

Greenwald, A.G. & Gillmore, G.M. (1997b). No pain, no gain? The importance of measuring course workload in student ratings of instruction. *Journal of Educational Psychology*, 89 (4), 743-751.

Groder, M. (1977). Groder's 5 OK diagrams. In G. Barnes (ed.), *Transactional analysis after Eric Berne: Teachings and practices of three TA schools*. New York: Harper's College Press.

Groder, M. (1980). *Business games: How to recognize the players and deal with them*, New York: Boardroom Books.

Groder, M. (1996). The fractionated nature of human nature. Presentation at the Annual meeting of the International Transactional Analysis Association, August, 1996, Calgary, Alberta, Canada.

Habermas, J. (1981). *The theory of communicative action: Reason and the rationalization of society*, Vol. 1. Boston: Beacon Press.

Haskell, R.E. (1997). Academic freedom, tenure, and student evaluation of teachers: Galloping polls in the 21st century. *Educational Policy Analysis Archives*, 5(6).

Harris, S. (2005). *The end of faith: Religion, terror, and the future of reason.* New York: W.W. Norton & Company.

Harris, T. (1967). *I'm OK—You're OK: A practical guide to transactional analysis.* New York: Harper & Row, Publishers.

Hastorf, A.H. and Isen, A.M. (1982). *Cognitive social psychology.* New York: Elsevier North Holland, Inc.

Healy, P. (2001). Harvard's quiet secret: Rampant grade inflation. *The Boston Globe*, October 7, 2001.

Hearn, C.G. (2002). *Tracks in the sea: Matthew Fontaine Maury and the mapping of the oceans.* Crawfordsville, IN: R. R. Donnelly.

Heathcote, A. (2006). Applying transactional analysis to the understanding of narcissism. *Transactional analysis journal,* 36(3), 228-234.

Hebb, D.O. (1949). *The organization of behavior: A neuropsychological theory.* New York: Wiley.

Hightower, J. (2003). *Thieves in high places: They've stolen our country and it's time to take it back.* Viking: New York.

Hine, Jenni (2005). Brain structures and ego states. *Transactional analysis journal,* Vol. 33, No. 1, pp. 40-51.

Hobbes, Thomas (1651). *Leviathan.* J.C.A. Gaskin, Ed. (USA: Oxford University Press, 1998).

Hume, David (1738) *A treatise of human nature,* Vol. I., London, J.M. Dent & Sons and in New York by E.P. Dutton & Co.

ITAA (1998). *Membership Directory of the International Transactional Analysis Association.* San Francisco, CA.

Hosmer, L.T., Cooper, A.C., & Vesper, K.H. (1977). *The entrepreneurial function: Text and cases on smaller firms.* Englewood Cliffs, NJ: Prentice Hall.

Jackson, P.W. (1977). Comments on CHAPTER 11 by Berliner and Rosenshine, in *Schooling and the acquisition of knowledge,* Anderson, R.C., Spiro, W.E., and Montague, W.E., (eds.). Hillsdale, N.J.: Lawrence Erlbaum Associates, Publishers.

Jacobs, A. (1991). Aspects of Survival: Triumph over death and onliness. *Transactional Analysis Journal.* 21(1). 4-11.

Jaffe, D.T. (1990). *Working with the ones you love: Conflict resolution and problem-solving strategies for a successful family business.* Berkeley, CA: Conari Press.

James, Muriel and Jongeward, D. (1973). *Born to win: Transactional analysis with gestalt experiments,* Reading, Mass: Addison-Wesley Publishing Co.

James, M. (1974). Self-Reparenting: Application to Script Analysis. *Transactional Analysis Journal.* 4(3) 32-39.

James, M. (1975). *The OK Boss.* Reading, Mass: Addison-Wesley Publishing Company.

Jongeward, D. (1973). *Everybody wins: Transactional analysis applied to organizations.* Menlo Park, CA: Addison-Wesley Publishing Company.

Johnson, R.A. and Wichern, D.W. (1999). *Applied multivariate statistical analysis.* Upper Saddle River, N.J.: Prentice Hall.

Johnson, V.E. (2002). An A is an A is an A . . . and that's the problem. *New York Times*, Section 4A, Page 14, Column 1.

Joines, V. and Stewart, I. (1987). *TA today: A new introduction to transactional analysis.* Nottingham and Chapel Hill: Lifespace Publishing.

Kahler, Taibi and Capers, Hedges (1974). The Miniscript. *Transactional Analysis Journal.* 4(1), 26-42.

Kant, Immanuel (1781) *Critique of pure reason*, second ed 1787, first published 1781, translated by Norman Kemp Smith, *Immanuel Kant's Critique of Pure Reason*, London: Macmillan & Co Ltd; New York: St. Martin's Press, 1963

Kao, J. (1989). *Entrepreneurship, creativity, & organization.* Englewood Cliffs, NJ: Prentice Hall.

Karpman, S. (1968). Fairy tales and script drama analysis, *Transactional Analysis Bulletin*. 7(26), 39 43.

Karpman, S. (1975). The bias box for competing psychotherapies. *Transactional Analysis Journal*, 5, 107-116.

Keynes, J.M. (1936). *The general theory of employment, interest, and money.* San Diego, CA: Harcourt Brace & Company, 1991.

Lankton, S.R. (1980). *Practical magic: A translation of basic neuro-linguistic programming into clinical psychology.* Cupertino, CA: Meta Publications.

Lea, J.W. (1991). *Keeping it in the Family.* New York: John Wiley & Sons.

LeDoux, J. (1994). Emotion, memory and the brain. *Scientific American, 270*(6), 50-57.

LeDoux. J. (1996). *The emotional brain: The mysterious underpinnings of emotional life.* New York: Touchstone Books.

LeDoux, J. (2002). *Synaptic Self: How our brains become who we are.* New York: Penguin Putnam.

Lloyd, S. (2006). *Programming the universe: A quantum computer scientist takes on the cosmos.* New York: Alfred A. Knopf.

Lord, R.G. and Kernan, M.C. (1987). Scripts as determinants of purposeful behavior in organizations. *Academy of management review,* Vol. 12, No. 2, 265-277.

Loria, B.R. (1991). Integrative family therapy: A constructivist perspective. In B.R. Loria (Ed.) *The Stamford papers: Selections from the 29th annual ITAA conference* (pp. 34-41). Madison, WI: Omnipress.

Kauffman. S.A. (1993). *The origins of Order: Self-Organization and Selection in Evolution,* New York: Oxford Univ. Press.

Malthus, Thomas (1798). *An Essay on the Principle of Population, as it Affects the Future Improvement of Society with Remarks on the Speculations of Mr. Godwin, M. Condorcet, and Other Writers.* London: Johnson.

Marx, Karl (1867). *Das kapital: A critique of political economy.* Chicago: Henry Regnery Company.

Maturana, H.R. and Varela, F.J. (1980*). Autopoiesis and cognition: The realization of living.* Dordrecht, Holland: D. Reidel Publishing Company.

Maturana, H.R. and Varela, F.J. (1987). *The tree of knowledge.* Boston: New Science Library.

Maury, D.H. (1894). *Recollections of a Virginian in the Mexican, Indian, and Civil Wars.* New York: Charles Scribner's Sons.

Maury, M.F. (1836). *A new theoretical and practical treatise on navigation.* Philadelphia: Key and Biddle.

Maury, M.F. (1855). *Physical geography of the seas.* New York: Harper & Brothers. Now available from amazon.com as *The physical geography of the seas and its meteorology.* Dover Publications, 2003.

McCulloch, W.S. (1988). *Embodiments of mind.* Cambridge: MIT Press, 1988.

McKenna, J. (1974). Stroking profile: Applications to script analysis, *Transactional Analysis Journal,* 4(4), 20-24.

Mieczkowski, B. (1991). *Dysfunctional bureaucracy: A comparative and historical perspective.* Lanham, Maryland: University Press of America.

Mieczkowski, B. (1995). *The rot at the top: Dysfunctional bureaucracy in academia.* Lanham, Maryland: University Press of America.

Moore, M. (2001). *Stupid white men and other sorry excuses for the state of the nation!* New York: HarperCollins Publishers, Inc.

Neisser, U. (1976). *Cognition and reality: Principles and implications of cognitive psychology.* W.H. Freeman and Company: San Francisco.

Nisbett, R. and Ross, L. (1980). *Human inference: Strategies and shortcomings of social judgment.* Englewood Cliffs, N.J.: Prentice-Hall, Inc.

Novey, Theodore (2002). Measuring the effectiveness of transactional analysis: An international study. *Transactional Analysis Journal,* 32: 1, pp. 8-25.

Osnes, R. (1974). Spot Reparenting. *Transactional Analysis Journal.* 4(3), 40-46.

Osnes, R. and Gesme, C. (2000). *Life is a celebration.* Edina, Minnesota: Beaver's Creek Press.

Pascal, B. (1669). *The Pensees (thoughts).* A defense of the Christian religion by Blaise Pascal, a renowned 17th century philosopher and mathematician. Wikipedia, the free encyclopedia. En.wikipedia.org/wiki/Pensees.

Perls, F. S. (1969). *Gestalt therapy verbatim.* Moab, Utah: The Real People Press.

Perls, F. (1969). *In and out of the garbage pail.* Moab, Utah: The Real People Press.

Piaget, J. (1971). *The grasp of consciousness.* Cambridge, Mass.: Harvard University Press.

Popper, K.R. and Eccles, J.C. (1977). *The self and its brain.* Berlin/ New York/London: Springer International.

Powers, R. (2006). *Mark Twain: A Life.* New York: Free Press.

Prince, G.M. (1970). *The practice of creativity: A manual for dynamic group problem solving.* New York: Collier Books.

Random House Dictionary of the English Language. (1967). Stein, Jess, Urdang, and Laurence, editors, New York: Random House.

Rawls, J. (1999). *A theory of justice.* Cambridge, Mass: Harvard University Press.

Ronstadt, R.C. (1985). *Entrepreneurship: Text, cases, and notes.* Dover, MA: Lord Publishing Company.

Russell, B. and North, A.N. (1910, 1912, 1913). *Principia Mathematica,* 3 Vols. Cambridge: At the University Press. Russell, B. (1959). *My philosophical development.* London: George Allen and Unwin; New York: Simon and Schuster.

Russell, B. (1967, 1968, 1969). *The autobiography of Bertrand Russell,* 3 vols. London: George Allen and Unwin; Boston and Toronto: Little Brown and Company (Vols 1 and 2); New York: Simon and Schuster (Vol. 3).

Schiff, A. L. and Schiff, J. (1971). Passivity. *Transactional Analysis Journal,* 1(1), 71-78.

Schrage, Harry. (1965). The R & D Entrepreneur: Profile of Success. *Harvard Business Review,* Vol. 43, Nov.-Dec., p. 56.

Schank, R.C. and Abelson, R.P. (1977*). Scripts, plans, goals, and understanding.* Hillsdale, New Jersey: Lawrence Erlbaum Associates, Publishers.

Schumpeter, J.A. (1934). *The theory of economic development: An inquiry into profits, capital, credit, interest, and the business cycle.* Cambridge, Mass: Harvard University Press.

Schumpeter, J.A. (1942). *Capitalism, socialism, and democracy.* New York: Harper & Brothers.

Schumpeter, J.A. (1951). *Imperialism and social classes.* New York: A.M. Kelly, Oxford, Blackwell.

Simon, H.A. (1957). *Administrative behavior* (1st ed.). New York: The Free Press.

Simon, H.A. (1997). *Administrative behavior: A study of decision-making processes in administrative organization (4th ed.).* New York: The Free Press.

Smith, A. (1776). *An inquiry into the nature and causes of the wealth of nations,* reprinted as *The Wealth of Nations* (New York: Modern Library, Inc., 1937).

Soros, G. (2006). *The age of fallibility: Consequences of the war on terror.* New York: Public Affairs.

Statesboro Herald (2006, September 18). Chambliss observes effects of global warming: Recent trip to Greenland gives

New Perspective. Statesboro, GA: Statesboro Publishing Company, p. 1.

Stapleton, R.J. (1970). *An analysis of rural manpower migration patterns in the South Plains region of Texas.* (Doctoral dissertation). Washington, DC: Department of Labor, Office of Manpower Evaluation and Research, National Technical Information Service (PB188048). file:///Users/richardstapleton/Downloads/31295004728316-2.pdf

Stapleton, R.J. (1976). *Managing creatively: Action learning in action.* Washington, D.C.: University Press of America.

Stapleton, R.J. (1978). The chain of ego states. *Transactional Analysis Journal.* 8(3), 215-219.

Stapleton, R.J. (1979a, April). The classroom de-gamer. *Transactional Analysis Journal.* 9(2), 145-146.

Stapleton, R.J (1979b). *De-gaming teaching and learning: How to motivate learners and invite Okness.* Statesboro, GA: Effective Learning Publications.

Stapleton, R.J. (1984). Implications of small business prospectuses developed by business students. In D. Ray

(Ed.) *Proceeedings of the 1984 Annual Meeting of the Southern Management Association*, pp. 228-230.

Stapleton, R.J. (1985). *The entrepreneur: Concepts and cases on creativity in business.* Lanham, Maryland: University Press of America.

Stapleton, R.J., & Murkison, G. (1988, October). Entrepreneurial learning and small business failure rates. *Proceedings* of the 24th Annual Meeting, The Institute of Management Sciences Southeastern CHAPTER, Myrtle Beach, SC.

Stapleton, R.J. (1989-1990). Academic entrepreneurship: Using the case method to simulate competitive business markets. *Organizational Behavior Teaching Review.* Vol. XIV, No. IV, pp. 88-104.

Stapleton, R.J. and Murkison, G. (1990). Scripts and entrepreneurship. *Transactional Analysis Journal*, Vol. 20, No. 3, July, pp. 193-197.

Stapleton, R.J. (1991). Game-freer teaching and learning; How to increase intellectual productivity in schools by decreasing psychological games. In B.R. Loria (Ed.) *The Stamford Papers:*

Selections from the 29th annual ITAA conference, pp. 250-267. Madison, WI: Omnipress.

Stapleton, R.J., Murkison, G., and Stapleton, D.C. (1993). Feedbackregardinga game-free case method process used to educate general management and entrepreneurship students. *Proceedings of the 1993 Annual Meeting of the Southeast CHAPTER of the Institute for Management Science.* Myrtle Beach, SC, October, 1993

Stapleton, R.J., Murkison, G., and Stapleton, D.C. (1994). Realistically estimating the magnitude and significance of business learning: Longitudinal feedback regarding a management learning process. *Manuscript.* Georgia Southern University.

Stapleton, R.J. and Stapleton, D.C. (1996). Randomly selecting students to lead case method discussions: Problems and pitfalls in performance appraisal. *Proceedings of the 1996 Annual Meeting of SE INFORMS,* Myrtle Beach, SC, October, 1996. This paper won the Best Paper Award for the Education Innovation Track at the conference.

Stapleton, R.J. and Price, B. (1997). Fall Quarter Student Evaluation Research Findings. *Manuscript.* Department of Management, Georgia Southern University.

Stapleton, R.J., Murkison, G., and Stapleton, D.C. (1997). The significance of schemata and scripts in entrepreneurship education and development. In T.G. Monroy, J. Reichert, F. Hoy, & K. Williams (Eds.), *The art and science of entrepreneurship education: Volume IV* (pp, 89-104). Akron, OH: The Project for excellence in Entrepreneurship Education.

Stapleton, R. J. (1998). *Business Voyages: Mental maps, scripts, schemata, and tools for finding and co-constructing your own business worlds*. Monograph. Statesboro, GA: Georgia Southern Printing Services.

Stapleton, R.J. and Stapleton, D.C. (1998). Teaching business using the case method and transactional analysis: A constructivist approach. *Transactional Analysis Journal*, 28(2), 157-167.

Stapleton, R. J. and Stapleton, D.C. (2001). Basic policies affecting the longevity of family businesses. *Proceedings* of the Annual Meeting of the Southeastern CHAPTER of Information Systems and Decision Sciences, Myrtle Beach, South Carolina.

Stapleton, R.J. and Murkison, G. (2001). Optimizing the fairness of student evaluations: A study of correlations between instructor excellence, study production, learning production, and expected grades. *The journal of management education*, 25(3), 269-292.

(Optimizing the Fairness of Student Evaluations has by now (April 5, 2021) been cited as a reference in 75 refereed journal articles in most academic disciplines. https://studysites. sagepub.com/holt/ articles/Stapleton.pdf)

Stapleton, R. J. and Stapleton, D. C. (2002). Attitudes of family business owners regarding policies for transferring the wealth of family businesses, *Proceedings* of the 26th Annual Conference, Small Business Institute Directors Association, February, San Diego, CA, pp. 172-177.

Stapleton, R.J. (2003). *Georgia southern entrepreneurship: Activities, contributors, cases (4th ed.).* Monograph. Statesboro, GA: Georgia Southern Printing Services.

Stapleton, R.J. and Stapleton, D.C. (2003a). The truth of student evaluations. Manuscript.

Stapleton, R.J. and Stapleton, D.C. (2003b). The morality of university grading. Manuscript.

Stapleton, R.J., Stapleton, D.C., & Tomlinson, M. (2004). Factors in family business planning. *Proceedings* of the Annual Meeting of the Small Business Institute Director's Association.

Clearwater Beach, FL, February. This article has been reprinted in several publications, including The Script, a publication of the International Transactional Analysis Association.

Stapleton, R.J. (2008) *Business Voyages: Mental Maps, Scripts, Schemata, and Tools for Discovering and Co-Constructing Your Own Business Worlds*, Statesboro, Georgia: Effective Learning Publications, Amazon.com., 712 pages. https://www.amazon. com/Business-Voyages-Schemata-Discovering-Co-Constructing/dp/1413480810

Stapleton, R.J. (2012) *Recommendations for Waking Up From the American Nightmare,* an eBook, Amazon.com., 253 pages. *https://www.amazon. com/Recommendations-American-Nightmare-Business-Voyages-ebook/dp/B009TOJVPI*

Stapleton, R.J. (2016) *Born to Learn: A Transactional* Analysis of Human Learning, Statesboro, Georgia: Effective Learning Publications, https://www. amazon.com/Born-Learn-Transactional-Analysis- Learning/dp/0692584331/ref=sr_1_1?ie=UTF8_&qid=1510510282&sr=8-1&keywords=born+to_+learn++++richard+john+stapleton&dpID=414yiE-4%252BIL&preST=_SY291_BO1,204,203,200_QL40_&dpSrc=srch

Stapleton, R.J. (2020) "The Evolution of Spaceship Earth, Inc.", *Effective Learning Report*, Statesboro, GA: Effective Learning Publications, https://blog. effectivelearning.net/the-evolution-of-spaceship-earth-inc-3/

Stevenson, H., Roberts, M., & Grousbeck, H. (1994). *New business ventures and the entrepreneur.* Burr Ridge, Ill.: Irwin.

Stevenson, H.H.; Grousbeck, H.I.; Roberts, M.J.; and Bhide, A. (1999). *New business ventures and the entrepreneur* (5th ed.). Boston: McGraw-Hill Irwin.

Steiner, C. (1971). The stroke economy. *Transactional Analysis Journal.* 1(3), 9-15.

Steiner, C. (1974). *Scripts people live: Transactional analysis of life scripts.* New York: Grove Press.

Steiner, C. M. (2003). Letter from the guest coeditor. *Transactional Analysis Journal.* 33(2), 111-114.

Stewart, I. and Joines, V. (1987). *TA Today: A new introduction to transactional analysis.* Nottingham and Chapel Hill: Lifespace Publishing.

The Economist (2001, April 12). All shall have prizes. London: Economist.com.

The Economist (2002, October 5). Who's been cheating? Exams are about sorting the bright from the dim, not about demonstrating progress, 365(8293).

The Economist (2006, September 15-19). The heat is on: A special report on climate change. London, 380(8494).

Thompson, A.A., & Strickland, A.J. (1987). *Strategic management: Concepts and cases.* Plano, TX: Business Publications, Inc.

Thompson, A. & Strickland, A. (1995). *Strategic management: Concepts and cases.* Chicago, Ill.: Irwin.

Thompson, A.A. & Strickland, A.J. (2003). *Strategic Management: Concepts and Cases* (13th ed.). Boston: McGraw-Hill Irwin.

Thorndyke, P.W. and Hayes-Roth, B. (1979). The use of schemata in the acquisition and transfer of knowledge. *Cognitive psychology,* Vol. 11, pp. 82-106.

Timmons, Jeffrey A. (1994*). New venture creation: Entrepreneurship for the 21st century.* Burr Ridge, ILL: IRWIN

Tocqueville, A. de (1835). *Democracy in America.* H. Reeve, trans., P. Bradley, ed., Everyman's Library, New York: Alfred A. Knopf, 1994.

Towl, A.R. (1969). *To study administration by cases.* Boston: Harvard University Press.

USAToday (2007, February 21). Pension tension: More and more retirees are finding it pays to have worked for the government instead of the private sector. McLean, VA; Gannett Company, Inc., p. 2A

Veblen, T. (1902). *The theory of the leisure class: An economic study of institutions.* New York: Macmillan.

Vesper, Karl H. (1996). *New venture experience: Text, exercises, cases.* Seattle, WA: Vector Books.

Von Foerster, Heinz (1984). "On constructing a reality", in *The invented reality: How do we know what we believe we know.* Paul Watzlawick (Ed.). New York: W.W. Norton & Company.

Von Glaserfeld, E. (1988). *The construction of knowledge: Contribution to conceptual semantics.* Salinas, CA: Intersystems Publications.

Wagner, Abe (1991). *Say it Straight or You'll Show it Crooked.* Denver, Colorado: Abe Wagner and Associates.

Walsh, D. (1985*). Selling out America's children.* Minneapolis: Fairview Press, 1994.

Ward, P.D. (2006, October). Impact from the deep: Strangling heat and gases emanating from the earth and sea, not asteroids, most likely caused several ancient mass extinctions. *Scientific American*, Vol. 295, No. 4, pp. 65-71.

Watzlawick, P. (1984). *The invented reality: How do we know what we believe we know?: Contributions to constructivism.* (P. Watzlawick, ed.). New York:
W.W. Norton & Company.

Weiner, J. (1995). *The beak of the finch: A story of evolution in our time.* New York: Alfred A. Knopf.

Wittgenstein, L. (1968). *Philosophical investigations* (G.E.M. Anscombe, trans.). Oxford: Basil Blackwell. First published in 1953.

Wittgenstein, L. (1971), *Prototractatus*, an early version of *Tractatus Logico-Philosophicus*, edited by B.F. McGuinness, T. Nyberg, and G.H. von Wright, with a translation by D.F. Pears and B.F. McGuinness with an historical introduction by G.H. von Wright and a facsimile of the author's manuscript. Ithaca, New York: Cornell University Press. First published in 1921.

Wood, J.D. and Petriglieri, G. (2005). Transcending polarization: Beyond binary thinking. *Transactional analysis journal*, Vol. 33, No. 1, pp. 31-39.

www.ingramcontent.com/pod-product-compliance
Lightning Source LLC
Chambersburg PA
CBHW031251160726
47993CB00001B/105